A Place to Belong

A PLACE TO BELONG

FAITH AND LOVE HOLD
GENERATIONS TOGETHER

TRACIE PETERSON

THORNDIKE PRESS

An imprint of Thomson Gale, a part of The Thomson Corporation

THOMSON
GALE

Detroit • New York • San Francisco • New Haven, Conn. • Waterville, Maine • London

THOMSON
━━━━★━━━ ™
GALE

LIBRARY OF CONGRESS CATALOGING-IN-PUBLICATION DATA

Peterson, Tracie.
  A place to belong : faith and love hold generations together / by Tracie Peterson. — Large print ed.
    p. cm. — (New Mexico sunrise ; no. 1) (Thorndike Press large print Christian fiction)
  Originally published in the work New Mexico sunrise. Uhrichsville, Ohio : Barbour Pub., 1993.
  ISBN 0-7862-9158-3 (hardcover : alk. paper) 1. Large type books. I. Title.
PS3566.E7717P57 2006
813'.54—dc22   2006026606

U.S. Hardcover:
ISBN 13: 978-0-7862-9158-8
ISBN 10: 0-7862-9158-3

Published in 2006 by arrangement with Barbour Publishing Inc.

Printed in the United States of America on permanent paper
10 9 8 7 6 5 4 3 2 1

Dear Readers,

I'm happy to tell you about the re-release of eight previously published **Heartsong Presents** romances. First issued under the name Janelle Jamison, this collection launched my fiction writing ministry.

New Mexico Sunrise is book one in a two-book collection that follows the lives of the Lucas, Monroe, and Dawson families.

I hope you'll enjoy the collection in this book, as well as the one which follows in book two, *New Mexico Sunset*. God bless you!

Tracie Peterson

CHAPTER 1

The Kansas heat was enough to wilt the sturdiest flower. Humid air hung thick and heavy, but certainly no heavier than the atmosphere inside the Intissar parlor on that June day.

"I won't go!" Magdelena Intissar announced at the top of her lungs. She stamped her small foot, just in case her words weren't enough to make her decision clear.

"Maggie, lower your voice," Sophia Intissar said patiently. The stately old woman was used to her granddaughter's temper. The only other person in the parlor was the subject of Maggie's displeasure.

"I won't go with that man, Grandmother. And that's final!" Maggie's blue eyes blazed at Garrett Lucas. He shifted uncomfortably.

Sophia smiled sympathetically at the young man. He had appeared on her door-step only hours earlier, and with him had come the news that Maggie's father was sending for his daughter.

With a swish of her English afternoon dress, Sophia moved gracefully to a chair and took her place. "I suggest you sit, Magdelena," she said, pointing to a brocade parlor chair. "This issue will not be easily dismissed. We must talk."

Maggie never took her eyes off Garrett Lucas as she followed her grandmother's instructions and sat down.

"Please continue, Mr. Lucas," Sophia requested.

"As I said, Ma'am," Garrett began. "Your son, Jason Intissar, instructed me to come to Topeka and return to New Mexico with his daughter. I have two train tickets." He pulled the tickets from his vest pocket and held them up for both women to see.

"So what! You have two train tickets," Maggie interrupted, enraged at the presumption that this should make any difference.

"Grandmother," she said, turning to Sophia Intissar. "You can't trust him. Anybody can buy train tickets. He's probably some kidnapper who thinks Father will pay a high price for my return."

Garrett chuckled, but Maggie ignored him.

8

"Grandmother, it wouldn't be appropriate for me to travel unchaperoned with this man. What would our friends say?" Maggie knew she was grasping at straws. Neither she nor her grandmother had ever given much thought to neighborhood gossip.

Sophia took the tickets, reviewed them, and returned them to Garrett Lucas's well-tanned hand.

"I also have this letter," Garrett said. Reaching into his pocket, he pulled out a sealed envelope.

Sophia took the letter and used it to fan herself for a moment. The high collar of her gown framed her thin, aged face. Signs of quality were evident from her gleaming white hair to the sweep of her elegantly tailored gown. Lifting her chin slightly, she drew a deep breath.

"I believe you are who you say you are, Mr. Lucas. I believe this letter will explain that my son has sent you to retrieve his daughter. We all know he's tried many times before. What I don't understand is why you must leave today on the four o'clock train."

"The letter will explain, Ma'am. Mr. Intissar was afraid his daughter might react as she had before and run off."

"How dare you!" Maggie could take no more. "How dare you talk about me as if I weren't even here! You don't know me. My father doesn't know me. He deserted me to my grandmother's care when my mother died. I was eight years old, and I've only seen him twice since then!" The bitterness in Maggie's voice was not lost on her listeners.

"Maggie, remember your manners," Sophia interjected firmly, but not without gentleness. She'd known the pain of that eight-year-old girl as she knew the pain of the young woman who sat angrily before her. "Mr. Lucas does have a point," she continued.

Maggie knew her grandmother was right. Her father had sent for her on a dozen other occasions, but Maggie had always managed to be away from Topeka or hiding out with friends when he had arrived to take her home. She'd never been able to get past the pain of being left behind, and in her heart, Maggie had held an anger toward her father that seemed to grow each year.

Now, Garrett Lucas had arrived. If she were forced to leave with him, Maggie knew it would not be easy to escape and return to her grandmother. But no matter how difficult flight might prove to be, Maggie was determined to defy her father's wishes. She had no desire to face him or the wounds that stood between them.

"It seems your father has outwitted you, my dear," Sophia was saying. Maggie jerked her head up.

"You'll have to drag my dead body to that train!" she shouted, jumping to her feet. Garrett's lips drew back in a wide grin. The girl had spunk, and he had to admire her ability to stand up to people.

Maggie noticed the smile and felt her heart skip a beat. Garrett Lucas was quite handsome, especially when he smiled. His skin was tanned from many years spent outdoors, and Maggie lost herself in his intense blue eyes. Just then she remembered he was grinning because of her.

Maggie raised herself to her full height. "I mean it. Go back and tell my father I refuse to come to New Mexico. I have friends and family here, and that's enough for me. Furthermore, in less than two months I will be eighteen years old. I think I am more than mature enough to make my own decisions, and my decision is to remain here."

As Maggie's tantrum played out, silence fell over the parlor. Sophia quietly read her son's letter. From time to time, a faint breeze fluttered the lace parlor curtains, bringing with it the sweet scent of honeysuckle.

Maggie refused to look at Garrett, but she was well aware that he studied her intently. How she wished she could run from the room.

Sophia let the letter fall to her lap. It confirmed that her son was determined to form a relationship with his child. Pity he'd allowed Maggie to have her way for so many years. There were so many miles and scars to overcome. But Maggie must face her father's decision. Scars or no scars, it was time for her to go home.

Sophia broke the silence. "Maggie, I have no choice. You will go with Mr. Lucas."

"What? You can't be serious, Grandmother. You would trust this man, this . . . this devil?"

"Magdelena!" Sophia admonished, and Garrett Lucas broke into a hearty laugh, causing both women to look at him.

"Excuse me, Ma'am," Garrett said to Sophia. "I meant no disrespect."

"I apologize for my granddaughter, Mr. Lucas. She doesn't yet understand that being grown up often means making unpopular and unwanted decisions."

Maggie came to stand in front of Sophia. "Grandmother, what are you saying? Will you really let him take me away?"

"Maggie, I must. Your father has made it

12

very clear in this letter. He has his reasons, and now I have mine. Run upstairs and pack your things."

"She doesn't need to take too much," Garrett offered. "Jason's bought her quite a bit already. She'll have enough clothes to be the envy of any woman in the territory."

"Clothes? Pack my clothes? Has everyone lost their minds?" Maggie questioned, her voice nearing hysteria. "What's in that letter? How could you send me off with a stranger to a man who cares nothing about me. He walked out on me, remember? He left me when I needed him."

"Maggie," Sophia took her granddaughter's youthful hand in her own weathered one and patted it gently. "You must be brave, my dear. You must listen to me and do as I say. I am an old woman, and I don't have many years left in this world. God is in this change."

"Don't say that," Maggie interrupted curtly. "God can't possibly care about me, or He'd have kept Garrett Lucas in New Mexico. God has never cared about me, or He would have given me a father. One that would stay and do the job, rather than leave it to someone else to do."

"Maggie, that's not fair. Please hear me out," Sophia pleaded, and Maggie grew

13

frightened. It wasn't at all like her grandmother to take on an air of frailty. Maggie's eyes darted in the direction of Garrett Lucas, but she could see he was fidgeting with his coat button, trying to leave the two women some privacy.

"I don't want you thinking I don't love you anymore. Nor do I wish for you to believe me cruel and heartless in this matter. You're seventeen years old, and your father feels it's time for you to consider marriage and settling down to your own family."

Sophia stopped to see the impact her words were having on Maggie. She could see tears brimming in her granddaughter's eyes and knew her own weren't far behind. "Your father has found a husband for you, Child. He has that privilege and right."

"A husband? I guess I could've guessed he didn't want a daughter. He just wants a son to replace the one he lost." Maggie's bitterness was clear.

"Now, Child, be fair," Sophia implored.

"What would I want with one of Father's old cronies? He probably has some ancient man lined up. I won't do it. I can't!" Maggie sobbed the words. She fell to her knees, hating herself for breaking down in front of Mr. Lucas.

"Child, you must understand. Your father is not a well man. The letter makes this clear. He wishes to leave his estate to you. And," Sophia added most reluctantly, "he wants to have a say in who will share that responsibility with you."

"Let him find someone to give his empire to. I don't want it. I want to stay here with you, Grandmother. I don't want to leave Topeka."

Just then the hall clock chimed two. Maggie turned terror-stricken eyes first to her grandmother, then unwillingly to Garrett Lucas.

Garrett hated being the cause of the fear he saw in Maggie's eyes. She was easier to handle when she was defiant. He wished he could assure her that he was only here as a favor to Jason, but he knew she'd never listen to him. No, it was best that he let the two women work through this together.

"If God loves me so much, why is He allowing this to happen? Better yet, why are you?" Maggie knew her words tortured her grandmother, but she had to make her grandmother see her pain.

"Maggie, I have little choice. I would love to have you here for the remainder of my life, but your father has set his mind."

"He doesn't care about me, Grandmother.

It's just his land and his business ventures. Don't you see? If he cared about me, he would have come home to Topeka. He wouldn't have jeopardized my security by forcing me away from all I know and love. He wants a land baron, not a daughter. He's always hated me for what happened to mother!"

"Nonsense, Child. You listen to me and listen well. I was there when your mother died. She struggled to give birth to your brother, but we all knew neither one of them was going to make it." Sophia's eyes clouded with tears.

"Typhoid fever had been fierce in town. Your mother was well into her pregnancy when you came down with the fever yourself. Before I knew what had happened, your mother was sick as well."

Maggie felt tears fall hot upon her cheeks. She buried her face in her grandmother's lap. Sophia gently stroked the long auburn curls. "Your father always blamed himself. He couldn't live with his grief nor with the child that reminded him so much of his wife. You were a constant reminder of what he had lost. I love my son, Maggie. I never faulted him for leaving you in my care. I saw the necessity of it then, just as I see the necessity of this now. God has always been

16

here for us."

"Father left because he blamed me for Mother's death. He hates me, and I don't care!" Maggie exploded.

"That is absurd, Maggie. You didn't give your mother typhoid, and your father didn't blame you then or now." Sophia lifted the letter to fan herself, succumbing to the heat and stress. Her face paled.

"Grandmother!" Maggie cried, reaching out to steady her. Garrett was beside Sophia in a moment.

"Get her some water," he commanded. Maggie raced to the kitchen and returned with a glass.

"It's not very cold," she said apologetically.

"It will be fine, Child," Sophia assured her. "I'm feeling better now. It's just this insufferable heat. If this is any indication of what the rest of the summer will bring, I'm not sure how I'll stand up under it."

"See, you need me," Maggie said pleadingly. Then she whirled to face Garrett. "You can't expect me to leave her here alone!"

Garrett was standing close to Maggie. Close enough she could smell the cologne he wore, musky, yet sweet. He looked down at her with soft eyes and opened his mouth to speak.

"It isn't my decision, Miss Intissar. I'm only doing what I promised your father I'd do."

"I'm fine, Maggie," Sophia insisted.

She did look better, Maggie decided, but the girl feared that neither of them would be able to bear the separation.

"I don't want to leave you." Maggie threw herself to her knees again and hugged her grandmother tightly.

Sophia brushed the damp hair away from Maggie's forehead. "I don't want to see you go. I love you, Child. But you must do this for me." Sophia raised Maggie's face to meet her own. "You must go with Mr. Lucas. Promise me you will go upstairs right now and pack your things."

Suddenly, there was no room for further discussion. Maggie stared intently at her grandmother's wearied face and then looked up at the towering stranger. She lowered her head and with a voice of complete dejection whispered, "Yes, Grandmother."

"And Maggie, remember God will always see you through the storms," Sophia added. "He's there for you Maggie, but you must come willingly. Don't put God off simply because you fear He will desert you. He won't." Sophia had prayed so often that her granddaughter would turn from her bitterness to accept Jesus as her Savior.

Maggie got to her feet and brushed off the skirt of her gown. "I will take my leave now, if I may," she said ignoring Garrett's closeness. Sophia nodded, and Maggie moved from the room.

As Maggie reached the oak staircase, she turned and made the mistake of meeting Garrett's unyielding eyes. Maggie sighed and began to climb the stairs, when a thought came to her. *Lillie! I'll sneak out of my room, down the trellis, and run to Lillie's house.* Maggie hiked her skirts and fairly flew up the remaining stairs. She was safely behind her bedroom door when Sophia Intissar rose slowly to her feet in the parlor below.

"If I know my granddaughter, Mr. Lucas, and I believe I do, I can count on her trying to leave this house without your knowledge. I would suggest you keep your eyes open. We have a staircase in back as well as the one in front."

Garrett nodded. "I understand. I'll keep track of her. You just rest." Garrett turned to leave, but Sophia placed her hand on his arm.

"Please be gentle with her, Mr. Lucas. Life

has not always treated her kindly."

"I'd venture a guess it's been rough on all of you. Please don't worry. I'll be a perfect gentleman. I'll do as Jason instructed me, and nothing more than is necessary to fulfill his wishes." With that, Garrett walked out the front door of the Intissar house.

CHAPTER 2

Maggie gazed around the room. She wondered if she should bother to take anything with her. No. She could always borrow clothes from Lillie. Nervous excitement washed through her body. It would be a pleasure to defeat Garrett Lucas and to show her father once again that she wanted nothing to do with him.

It was odd how days, even weeks, passed when Maggie didn't think of her father. God, on the other hand, could never be outrun.

Putting such uncomfortable thoughts aside, Maggie went to the window. She touched the powder-blue Priscilla curtains and remembered making them with her grandmother. Maggie held the soft folds against her cheek. She thought of how she and Grandmother had gone downtown to pick out the material and wallpaper for their new home in Potwin Place.

Maggie threw open the window. "I won't be forced to give up all that I love. It's just not fair!" she cried out loud. "Father can't force me to leave Grandmother and marry someone I don't know."

There was a light rap at the door. "Maggie, do hurry along, Child. We've only a few minutes before we leave," her grandmother called softly.

"In a minute," Maggie responded. She hurriedly reached out the window to take hold of the trellis. Her skirts were quite cumbersome as she struggled to put her foot out the window. Gingerly, Maggie climbed onto the delicate wood frame sharing space with the climbing roses. The trellis shook vigorously for a few moments, then settled under her weight.

"If he thinks that he can just come in here and take me away, he's got another think coming," Maggie muttered to herself as she fought her skirts and the trellis. "He's got to be twelve kinds of a fool to think I'd go anywhere with —" Her tirade ended abruptly as she was wrenched from the trellis into the arms of Garrett Lucas.

A look of amusement played in Garrett's eyes, and Maggie couldn't help but notice how effortlessly he carried her, squirming and twisting, back to the front door. "You

22

were saying?" he questioned sarcastically.

"Oh, you are insufferable! Put me down!" Maggie said, suddenly finding her voice.

Garrett carried her through the etched glass double doors of her Queen Anne home. He took the stairs two at a time and didn't stop until he reached the upstairs hallway.

"Which room?" he questioned.

"Put me down! Grandmother!" Maggie yelled.

"Unless you want me to help you pack, I suggest you settle down and do what your grandmother told you to do. I'm going to be watching this house the whole time, so no more tricks. Do you understand?" Garrett's words left Maggie cold. "Do you?"

Maggie nodded slowly.

"Very well," Garrett said as he set Maggie on her feet. "Now get your things together and be quick about it, or I'll come in and help you!" With that he went downstairs and left Maggie to watch after him in total amazement. Who was this man?

Maggie hurried to the sanctuary of her room. There was no more time for memories or escapes. If she couldn't get away from Garrett at home in Topeka, would it be possible to flee while on the train?

Suddenly, a plan began to form. "If Father

thinks he's won this round, he's wrong." Maggie said, pulling out a drawer from her writing desk. She dumped the contents onto the desktop. Coins and trinkets spilled out. "I'll show him," Maggie muttered to herself as she counted the money. Finally, thirty dollars and some change was counted out. "I wonder if this is enough to buy a train ticket home," Maggie mused.

Next, she pulled out a piece of writing paper and jotted a note to her best friend, Lillie Johnston. She tried to explain what was happening and that, somehow, she'd be back. She sealed the envelope and left it in the middle of her desk, knowing her grandmother would find it and have it delivered.

Quickly, Maggie pulled off her gingham day dress and took out a green linen traveling suit. The day was too hot for such an outfit, but Maggie knew it would be expected by the matrons of society.

Maggie herself often scoffed at the rules and regulations that the women of Potwin Place had made for themselves. But they were rules that were followed by the genteel of society everywhere, not just those in this upper-class neighborhood.

Maggie pulled on her petticoat, then eyed herself in the mirror. She was only seventeen, not even an adult. Still, many of her friends were already married. Some even had children. She was woman enough she decided, but for what?

She labored with her shirtwaist and the faux lace collar that tied at her neck. Securing the collar with a velvet green ribbon, Maggie turned her attention to the skirt.

Within twenty minutes, Maggie stood at the base of the oak staircase, dressed in her green suit with valise and purse in hand. She was an alluring picture with her long auburn hair put up and a green hat pinned jauntily to one side.

Her appearance was not lost on Garrett. "Let me take that, Miss Intissar," he said as he stepped forward to take the valise from Maggie's hands. Maggie glared at him but said nothing. He took the bag and stepped back.

"You must be stronger than you look. This thing weighs more than a yearling heifer," he drawled.

"I am a great many things more than what I appear to be, Mr. Lucas," Maggie answered, refusing to allow him the upper hand.

"Somehow, Ma'am, that doesn't surprise me." His eyes pierced her soul, and Maggie felt as though she'd just been put in her place.

"Oh good, you're here at last," Sophia said as she entered the room carrying another small bag. "I had Two Moons pack you some things to eat." Sophia referred to her Indian housekeeper who had been with her since she'd been a young girl.

"That isn't necessary, Ma'am," Garrett began. "Mr. Intissar sent along plenty of money for the two of us to eat along the way."

Maggie thought of at least a dozen retorts but kept her tongue in check for a time longer. Once they were on the train, Garrett Lucas would discover just how difficult his trip was going to be.

"I only thought you might need something extra. I suppose it's the mothering instinct in me." Sophia started to discard the bag, but Maggie reached out and took it.

"Nonsense, Grandmother. It was a wise idea," she said gently, while flashing a look at Garrett Lucas that made it clear he'd overstepped his bounds. "One can never tell when the food will be unsatisfactory. Why, Lillie told me just last week the food offered on their trip to Omaha had been appalling."

"Of course, Ma'am. It was very thoughtful of you." Garrett spoke politely, all the while returning Maggie's blazing stare. He

26

raised one dark eyebrow slightly, as if contemplating a further reply, then changed his mind. "I suggest we be on our way. It's already three o'clock."

"Very well, Mr. Lucas." Sophia allowed him to take her arm and lead her to the carriage.

Maggie lingered for a moment, trying to drink in every inch of the house. Standing at the foot of the stairs, she could look into three different rooms. They held comfort and good memories. Suddenly, she wanted to embrace it all, fearing that she'd never see her home again. Why was God punishing her? Hadn't she paid enough?

Maggie choked back tears and steadied her nerves. She'd make it back, she vowed to herself. All the Garrett Lucases and Jason Intissars in the world would not keep her from her home and Grandmother.

"Come along, Maggie." It was Grandmother calling from the carriage.

Maggie stepped onto the porch and shut the door behind her. She turned to find Garrett Lucas at her arm.

"I would suggest, Miss Intissar, that you make this matter as easy on your grandmother as possible." Garrett's voice was deadly serious. "She has done nothing but care for you and love you. You are a spoiled and selfish child." He paused to search her eyes. "I will not allow you to cause her further grief by a display of childishness at the train station."

Maggie's mouth dropped open in shocked surprise. "How dare you —" Her words were cut off by his stern expression.

"I'm not the enemy here, but you are going to get on that train if I have to rope you and tie you to the seat. Everyone, including that sweet, old woman, has danced to your tune long enough. You are now in my care, Miss Magdelena Intissar, and I am quite capable of dealing with you."

Maggie was stunned. She could barely work her legs to walk down the porch steps. It wouldn't be as easy to give Garrett Lucas the slip as she'd hoped. Mutely, Maggie allowed Garrett to lead her along the board walkway to the carriage.

Topeka of 1888 was bustling with life and activity. It was the capital of Kansas and in its own right demanded grandeur and charm. Potwin Place was the high point of residential Topeka, although it desired to become a city in its own right.

Potwin Place homes, while fairly new, were elegant and stately. They were surrounded by well-manicured lawns. Young trees had been planted along the avenues.

Maggie was well aware she had lived a privileged life. Now she could only stare longingly as the carriage took her from the place she loved to an uncertain future.

Maggie had always loved the hubbub of the city, but even that simple pleasure was lost on her as she brooded about the future. The carriage passed the large stone church which Sophia insisted her household attend every Sunday. Maggie thought momentarily of God. He was up there somewhere, she decided as she looked into the fluffy clouds. Somewhere up there, but certainly not with her.

Soon, the two-story depot came into sight. Maggie realized the moment of truth was nearing. She toyed with the idea of causing a scene. Maybe there was some way to discredit Mr. Lucas so that her grandmother couldn't possibly send Maggie with him.

Maggie shot a quick glance at Garrett Lucas. He narrowed his eyes slightly as if reading her mind. The look on his face was adamant, his message unmistakable.

"I must say, Mrs. Intissar, you have a lovely city," Garrett observed, breaking the silence that had lasted the duration of the carriage ride.

Sophia roused herself. "Yes, I suppose it is one of the more lovely times to be here.

The flowering trees, the honeysuckle and lilacs. Topeka is a sweet smelling town. However, we have some nasty storms. Cyclones, you know." She spoke with a heavy voice, and both Garrett and Maggie knew her mind was far from thoughts of the weather.

"Yes, Ma'am," Garrett replied, "We have them out West, too. Sometimes they come in a series of storms that last all day."

Sophia nodded. "I've seen storms like that. It's always been the thing I've disliked most about our fair state. Of course," she added rather absentmindedly, "if not cyclones, then something else."

Maggie sat in silence, trying to formulate a plan. There'd only be one chance to make it work. She thought of the various junctions and water stops on the Atchison, Topeka, and Santa Fe Rail Road lines. She'd traveled with her grandmother as far as Newton, but beyond that, she was rather uncertain about the route. She'd have to escape before they reached Newton.

The carriage ride came unceremoniously to an end at the depot entrance. Garrett jumped to the ground before the driver could announce their arrival.

"Allow me to help you, Ma'am," Garrett said tenderly, reaching up to take hold of

Sophia's waist. "Forgive the familiarity, but I fear this heat might grieve you if I allow you to exert yourself."

"You are very kind, Mr. Lucas. My son has always been a good judge of a man's character. I see his judgment is still sound."

Maggie rolled her eyes, not realizing that Garrett could see her. "Yes, Father is quite knowledgeable about men and horseflesh, cattle and land grants. It's women who seem to escape his understanding," she said sarcastically. She refused to take Garrett's offered hand and nearly fell from the buggy as she tried to dismount.

Garrett flashed her a brief smile and returned his attention to Sophia. The heat was nearly unbearable for the older woman.

"June isn't always this hot. Some years, we're still enjoying cool temperatures at this time. Why by all the means of Kansas, we could be quite chilled tomorrow. We have a saying about the weather here, Mr. Lucas, if you don't like it, wait a day and it'll change," Sophia murmured. She stumbled slightly, leaning heavily against Garrett's offered arm.

"Ma'am, I know you wish to see your granddaughter safely on the train, but the truth is it would be better if your driver took you home. I don't want to worry about you

31

having to make it back to the carriage without help." Garrett's command of the moment went unquestioned. Sophia allowed him to place her back in the buggy.

"Maggie, listen to me," Sophia said leaning down from her seat. "Don't cause Mr. Lucas any trouble. Just do as your father wishes, and perhaps in the fall, I'll come and visit you."

Maggie felt tears on her cheeks. She hated appearing weak in front of Garrett, but perhaps it was what he needed to see. He should understand how miserable he was making her.

"Grandmother, I simply can't bear to leave you." Maggie began to cry. "I don't want to go." She held tightly to her grandmother's arm.

"It will be alright, Child," Sophia murmured, gently stroking Maggie's face. "God sometimes sends adversity to strengthen and teach us. You'll grow stronger from this. Now remember the things you've been taught. Never forget you are loved."

"I'll remember," Maggie promised.

"It's time to go, Miss Intissar," Garrett said softly, extending his arm for Maggie.

"I'll see you soon, Grandmother," Maggie said standing on tiptoe in order to reach her Grandmother's ear. "I'll pray every night that God will bring us together again." She wondered if she had added that last statement more for herself than for her grandmother.

Maggie allowed Garrett to lead her away. As they passed through the depot entrance, she paused to look back. Her grandmother was waving weakly. Maggie returned the wave until Garrett firmly propelled her to the other side of the depot and onto the boarding platform.

Oh, Grandmother, Maggie thought. *Somehow I will return to you. Somehow.*

CHAPTER 3

"All 'board!" the conductor called as a stern-faced Garrett approached, pulling a willful Maggie behind him.

"Afternoon to you, Mister," the conductor said without breaking his concentration on the pocket watch he held tightly in his hand. "Missus," he added, touching the brim of his blue cap. Maggie stiffened at the comment, causing a smile to play at the corners of Garrett's mouth.

Maggie tried to pull away, but it was no use. Garrett only smiled broadly, and raised a questioning eye from beneath his black Stetson.

"Tickets, please," the conductor requested.

Garrett pulled two tickets from his vest pocket and handed them to the older man.

"Um, I see here you're in number fourteen. That'd be the second car down," the conductor said, motioning to a porter.

"Y'sir," the porter said with a nodding bow of his head.

"These passengers have seats in number fourteen. See to it," the conductor instructed. "And be quick about it. I'm about to call final 'board.'"

"Y'sir," the porter smiled and offered his assistance. "Do you have bags, Sir?" he questioned Garrett.

"I've already checked them," Garrett answered. "Except for this one. We'll take it with us." Garrett motioned to the carpetbag Sophia had packed. Maggie clutched the bag as if it were all she owned.

"Very good, Sir. Right this way."

Maggie felt herself being pulled along at such a pace that when Garrett stopped, she nearly fell headlong onto the tracks. Garrett steadied her and gently handed her up the steps of the train. Maggie was amazed at how light his touch could be when he wasn't bullying her along.

The porter led them down the narrow train aisle. "Seats twenty-three and twenty-four, right here, Sir," the porter said. "I'll show you to your sleeping compartments this evening."

"Thank you," Garrett replied, handing the man a coin. The porter smiled broadly and nodded his head to the couple.

"Take the window seat, Miss Intissar," Garrett stated matter-of-factly. "I believe the train is about to pull out, and it would do little good to have you sprawled in the aisle."

Maggie stepped meekly to her seat. Garrett, although surprised, said nothing. Instead, he took off his hat and coat and, before sitting, removed his vest as well. Maggie's discomfort became evident as Garrett pulled his necktie off and unbuttoned his shirt collar.

Garrett noticed Maggie's flushed face. She quickly turned away, and he couldn't help but grin. "I'm finished, if that's what you're wondering," he teased. "It'd do you some good to get out of that jacket and open up a button or two yourself."

"I'm fine for the time being," she lied, wishing she could do just as Garrett had suggested. The worst heat of the day was only heightened by the closed, cramped quarters of the train.

"As you wish, but remember we're traveling south. The heat will only get worse once we leave Topeka," Garrett said with a shrug of his shoulders.

His words only reminded Maggie that they were leaving her home. A further reminder sounded loud and clear as the

36

train whistle gave two long blasts. Maggie felt the color drain from her face. It was all she could do to keep from fighting Garrett in an attempt to get off.

The train gave a bit of a jerk, as if it needed help to start moving down the tracks. Finally, it started pulling slowly out of Topeka's Santa Fe Station. Maggie watched as people on the platform waved. One older woman, sending a kiss with her gloved hand, reminded Maggie of her grandmother. Maggie bit her lip to keep from crying, but her eyes held betraying tears.

Long after there was nothing but outlying farms and scenery to look at, Maggie continued to stare out the window. She remembered several years earlier when she had gone with Lillie to see the circus. The two girls had watched the animals get loaded on the train after the final performance. Maggie had felt sorry for the animals in their barred cages. Now, she felt caged.

After nearly fifteen minutes of strained silence, Garrett spoke. "We should talk before this situation gets worse," he began. He leaned back against the padded leather of the seat and crossed his arms behind his head.

Maggie stiffened and moved closer to the

window. She was hot and sticky, and the humidity made it nearly impossible to breathe. She wanted to lower the window, but the smoke and cinders from the train's smokestack would only worsen things. Either way, Garrett Lucas was too close, and she wished desperately to put some kind of distance between them. She sighed deeply.

"Did you hear what I said?" Garrett questioned.

"I heard you," Maggie barely whispered the words. "I simply chose not to argue with you."

"I have no intention of arguing with you, Miss Intissar, and begging your pardon, but I believe I will call you by your first name." Garrett's voice told Maggie he'd settle for nothing less.

"Whatever you feel is necessary, Mr. Lucas," Maggie replied with a coolness to her voice that surprised even her. "It is of little consequence what name you call me by."

"Dare I believe you are offering to cooperate with me?" Garrett questioned sarcastically. He turned his body slightly toward Maggie, which only made her more uncomfortable.

A woman with two children occupied the seats across the aisle, and she leaned toward

Garrett and Maggie to catch pieces of their conversation. Maggie detested the woman's prying attitude and lowered her voice even more.

"I've already agreed to go with you to wherever it is my father calls home. I don't care what you call me, and I don't care where you take me. Now, what more is there to discuss?" Maggie felt rather proud of her little speech.

"I see. What, may I ask, brought about this change in the wild-eyed child that I had words with earlier?" Garrett questioned, intently studying Maggie for some clue as to what she was planning.

Maggie bit hard on her lower lip, and Garrett smiled, letting Maggie know he was aware he'd hit a nerve.

"You have your father's temper. Are you aware of that?" Garrett asked. Maggie said nothing, but she noticed over Garrett's shoulder that the woman had leaned even farther into the aisle. Garrett turned to see what Maggie was looking at.

"Have you lost something, Ma'am?" Garrett asked the embarrassed woman. The woman shook her head and quickly turned her attention back to her children. Garrett chuckled and continued his analysis of Maggie.

"You have his eyes too." Garrett's voice sounded low and melodic. Maggie felt herself relaxing against her will.

"I suppose one would have to share certain characteristics with one's parent. It isn't necessary to live with a parent to look like one. I also look a great deal like my mother, and she died nine years ago," Maggie said rather stiffly, refusing to fall under Garrett's spell.

"Yes, I know. Your father showed me her picture. She was a beautiful woman, and you are the very image of her."

"Am I mistaken, or have you just complimented me?" Maggie questioned curiously.

"And the lady is intelligent too!" Garrett drawled sardonically.

Maggie could no longer play her part. "You're insufferable!" she huffed and turned back to the window.

"Ah ha! I knew the temper was still there. Don't think that you can set my mind at ease by playing the prim and proper lady. I will not trust you on this trip, and you might as well know my terms right up front," Garrett said firmly.

Maggie stared incredulously as Garrett sat up and reached over to pull her to the edge of her seat.

"Now, off with the jacket before you pass

out. And take off that collar," he ordered. He reached out as if to undo the buttons himself.

Maggie noticed the widening eyes of the woman across the aisle. Garrett turned to the woman briefly. "I can't believe you women actually travel comfortably in these getups you call traveling clothes." The woman turned crimson, but Maggie noticed she didn't pull back like before.

"Take it off," Garrett commanded a stunned Maggie.

"I've never been so insulted!" Maggie tried to jerk away, only to find Garrett's firm hands holding her upper arms.

"I'm sure no one has ever dared to cross you, Maggie. But this time, you've met your match. Your father didn't send me without considering the type of person this job required. Now do as I say." Garrett loosened his grip as Maggie obediently began to unbutton her jacket.

"This is totally inappropriate," she muttered under her breath. "I'm a lady, and I demand that you treat me as such."

"Perhaps when you start acting like one, I'll be more inclined to treat you differently. Fashion or no, I can't see having you passed out from heat. I'm truly thinking only of your comfort. Now let me help." Garrett's words were so precise they sounded rehearsed.

Maggie allowed him to help her out of the traveling jacket. She had to admit, at least to herself, it was an immediate improvement. She leaned back and sighed. Why was this happening? Did God hate her so much? Why couldn't she live with her grandmother? Was it because she refused to hear God's calling?

"Now, as I said before, we really should talk." Garrett's voice intruded into Maggie's thoughts. "I know you're feeling badly. I know you don't want to go, and I know that you're afraid."

"I'm not afraid of anything!" Maggie exclaimed, raising her voice slightly. When several of the train passengers joined the nosy woman in turning to see what the commotion was, Maggie immediately stared out the window.

"You were saying," Garrett whispered pressing close to her ear.

"Get away from me," Maggie hissed. "I may have to suffer through your deplorable presence, but I will not have you accosting me."

Garrett laughed loudly, causing people to stare at them once again. The woman across the aisle was thoroughly enjoying the scene.

"Will you be quiet?" Maggie whispered angrily. "I won't have the entire train watching me. One nanny is entirely too many, but now you'd saddle me with a dozen more," she said, waving her arm at the people who stared. Everyone, with the exception of the nosy woman, turned away quickly.

"Look, little girl," Garrett said in the authoritative tone Maggie had grown to hate. "You're spoiled and selfish, and a woman, you're not!"

Maggie felt her face grow red with embarrassment. Garrett Lucas was impossible. It made thoughts of escape seem that much sweeter. She struggled to regain her composure.

"Mr. Lucas," Maggie began when she could trust her voice. "I am tired of your insults and tired of trying to make sense out of this situation. I don't suppose it's possible for you to understand what I'm going through, therefore I don't see any reason to continue this conversation."

"Maybe I understand more than you give me credit for," Garrett answered gently.

"I suppose anything is possible," Maggie said wearily. "But I don't believe you appreciate my position. I am seventeen years old. I've lived all my life in Topeka. What few friends I have are ones I've spent a

43

lifetime making.

"Why, Lillie Johnston from next door has been my companion since I was a very small child. Her father and mine invested in the railroad together. Her parents and mine were good friends. When Lillie's parents decided to build a house in Potwin Place, my grandmother arranged to build there so we could remain close. I was to be in Lillie's wedding later this month. So you see how little you or my father know about me."

"I've learned a great deal about you through your grandmother's letters to your father," Garrett said noting the surprise on Maggie's face.

"I see," Maggie replied, knowing that her grandmother had written long, detailed accounts of their life in Topeka. Maggie decided that by sharing those letters with a stranger, her father had betrayed the family once again.

"I know that, except for times when Lillie prodded you to attend social events, you've lived a cloistered life," Garrett continued, much to Maggie's dismay. "I know that you've refused gentleman callers, telling your grandmother that men were more trouble to deal with than they were worth."

Maggie blushed a deep crimson. "My father had no right to share that with you.

In fact, my grandmother had no right to share it with my father. But," she paused, gaining a bit of composure, "I suppose that is all in the past."

"Your father has every right to know about you. He's tried for years to get you down to New Mexico with him. Seems to me that it's you, not him, who refuses to put the past aside. I can't imagine a living soul disliking Jason Intissar, much less hating him the way you do." Garrett's words were like a spike driven into Maggie's heart.

"You have no right to talk to me like that! I demand that you have the porter show me to my sleeping compartment so I might retire for the evening."

"I see. And if I refuse?" Garrett questioned in a cautious tone.

"I can't very well force you, now can I? I am, after all, just a spoiled little girl. But, I am not feeling well, and I am asking you," Maggie continued at nearly a whisper, "to let me go."

Maggie hoped her case sounded believable, but just in case, she quietly held her breath, a trick she and Lillie had learned as young girls. If she held her breath long enough, she'd grow faint. She and Lillie had done this on more than one occasion to get out of school. If Garrett expected childish behavior, then that's what she'd give him.

Garrett eyed her suspiciously. She was incredibly beautiful and looked nothing like the child he'd accused her of being. He liked her spirit, but he had to admit that she didn't look well.

"Alright, Maggie." Garrett agreed and signaled for the porter.

"Sir?" It was the same porter who'd shown them to their seats.

"Please show Miss Intissar to her sleeping compartment. I'm afraid the heat's been difficult for her," Garrett said as he stood and helped Maggie to her feet.

Maggie slowly exhaled but found herself dizzy from her antics. She fell against Garrett's arm. The woman across the aisle gasped loudly, but Garrett ignored her.

"Maggie?" he questioned, quite concerned. Maggie kept her face down and smiled to herself. *Good,* she thought. *Let him worry.*

"I'm so sorry," Maggie said aloud. "I'm afraid I'm feeling worse than I thought."

"Porter, lead the way. I'll bring Miss Intissar," Garrett directed, and the porter headed in the direction of the sleeping car. Garrett pulled Maggie tightly to him. "Lean on me, Maggie. I'll help you."

The fact that Maggie willingly accepted

his help caused Garrett great concern. She would never allow him to touch her if she were strong enough to do otherwise. When they reached Maggie's room, Garrett instructed the porter to bring fresh water and a glass.

"I want you to drink this," Garrett said to Maggie as he poured the glass full of water. "Then I want you to undress and get some rest."

Maggie raised an eyebrow this time. "You seem intent on speaking on very familiar terms with me. I'd rather you leave this relationship as unfamiliar as possible. Neither one of us has anything to gain by doing otherwise."

"On the contrary, Maggie. We have a great deal to gain by working through this antagonism — if not for our sakes, then for the sake of your father," Garrett replied as he pushed the glass into Maggie's hand.

Garrett's fingers touched Maggie's hand and sent a searing charge up her arm. She made the mistake of looking into his eyes. They were steely blue, and yet there was something more. They seemed to hold a glint of something that Maggie couldn't quite comprehend.

She pulled away from his hand and the glass of water. "Wha . . . what?" she stammered. "What could this possibly have to do with my father, and why should I care?"

"Because your father has gone to a great deal of trouble for you. He cares very deeply for you, and he wants your happiness," Garrett said, placing the water on the dresser of Maggie's compartment. "And, despite what you may think, his plans for you are better than your own."

Maggie stamped her foot. "My father doesn't even know me, Garrett Lucas! He's making arrangements for me to wed a man I don't know. A man who doesn't know me or what I care about in life."

"Your father knows more about you than you give him credit for, Maggie," Garrett stated as he walked to the door. "And, I might add, so does the man he's chosen to be your husband."

Maggie grew furious at this. "And just how would you know?" she asked, crossing her arms in front of her.

"Because, Maggie," Garrett replied dryly. "I am that man."

CHAPTER 4

Garrett returned to his seat with the porter close behind him. "Will you be needin' anything else, Sir?" the porter asked in a low voice.

"No, thank you," Garrett replied rather distracted.

"What about your missus, Sir?"

"No. Nothing." Garrett stated firmly.

When the porter had walked away, Garrett punched his fist against his leg.

I never should have told her like that, he thought. He stared out the window at the open expanse of Kansas grasslands flashing by. The train was traveling at nearly seventeen miles an hour.

Garrett closed his eyes and remembered Maggie's expression as he had told her that she was to marry him. Her look of terror had done little to assure him that he was doing the right thing.

Things had seemed much simpler back

on Jason Intissar's ranch. His mind flashed back to the day Maggie's portrait had arrived. Jason was intensely proud of his little girl, as he always referred to Maggie, but Garrett had seen a woman behind the little girl's eyes.

"She's a beauty, but wild, like a green-broke mustang," Jason had announced as both men studied the portrait. Maggie had put up quite a fight over the portrait sitting, agreeing to it only after Jason had given his word that she could stay another year with her grandmother.

The promised year had come and gone. Throughout the weeks and months, Jason and Garrett had found themselves paying homage to the portrait. Garrett remembered the day Jason had found him in the library studying his daughter's likeness.

"I've had some time to reflect on matters," Jason had begun. "It seems to me that a ranch the size of mine will need more than a wisp of a girl to run it. I've worked hard to train you in every area of my holdings. Seems only fitting that you reap the reward."

"Meaning?" Garrett had questioned.

"Meaning Maggie. She'll need a strong man. A good man. A Christian man." Garrett had said nothing, afraid to believe what he was hearing. Jason had continued, "I

50

want you to marry Maggie. That is, if what I think I've read in your eyes is true. You do love her, don't you?"

Garrett had found the thought startling, almost unsettling. But he'd known it was true. Everything Garrett had learned about Maggie in her grandmother's letters had filled him with a growing love.

"It won't be easy," Jason had explained. "She has a temper to beat all, and she won't take lightly to my choosing a husband for her."

Garrett had agreed to Jason's plan, certain that, in time, Maggie would come to feel for him the love he already felt for her.

The blast from the train whistle brought Garrett back to reality. Indeed, Maggie hadn't liked the idea of her father choosing either a husband or a home for her.

Garrett could understand Maggie's pain, but not her hatred. From their first encounter when Garrett was only fifteen, Jason had never been anything but kind to him. He had looked past the angry, pain-filled young man and seen potential that Garrett hadn't known existed. There was a kindness about Jason that brought people from the farthest reaches of the New Mexico Territory to seek work or assistance. Having known what it was to be in need, Jason never failed to feed

51

the hungry or help the hurting.

Jason had been successful in a little bit of everything, and Garrett couldn't think of a wealthier man in the territory. Knowing that he was dying, Jason's fondest wish was to leave his empire to the two people he loved most, Maggie and Garrett.

Garrett sighed. "I can't blame her for hating me. Jason and I knew this wasn't going to be love at first sight."

Garrett hated the thought of hurting Maggie, and yet he'd had to create an attitude of uncompromising firmness between them. He'd had to act the ruffian and cad in order to drag her from the care of her beloved grandmother. But Garrett was determined to bring Maggie back to Jason and put an end to her father's continued heartbreak.

Garrett glanced at his watch. Soon they'd be stopping for supper. At least Fred Harvey's restaurants, known as Harvey Houses, were at virtually every major stop on the rail.

Garrett remembered past meals with fond satisfaction. Fred Harvey allowed only the finest foods to be served in his restaurants. So meticulous was Harvey that he had water hauled in steel tank cars to every restaurant. Harvey had announced that this way, no matter where one traveled on the Santa Fe line, the coffee would taste the same. A wise decision, Garrett surmised, knowing the farther west they traveled, the heavier the alkali content in the water.

The car door opened, admitting the conductor. He announced loudly their arrival in Florence, the supper stop. Those who planned to dine in the Harvey House had given their meal choices to the porter back in Emporia. Their selections had been wired ahead and would be waiting, piping hot, for them to eat.

Garrett sighed. As much as he hated the idea of disturbing Maggie, leaving her alone on the train was out of the question. She was likely to run away as she had other times when Jason had sent for her.

Meanwhile, Maggie was pacing in her sleeping compartment, ranting and raging against her father, Garrett, and even God.

"The arrogance! The absurdity! If my father thinks for one minute that I'll allow him to marry me off to the likes of Garrett Lucas, he's out of his mind!" she shouted. She grabbed her glass of water and threw it against the door.

When her tantrum had played itself out, Maggie sat down on the edge of the bed. The entire room was only a few feet across and eight feet long. There was a window, a bowl and pitcher sitting on a tiny dresser, and a small wooden commode. The bed itself was barely wide enough for one person, and Maggie wondered if her feet would hang over the edge.

She sat in silence for a long while and contemplated Garrett's final words. He was to be her husband! "Oh God," she breathed. "Why do You hate me so?"

A clouded memory appeared. Her mother's loving face bent over her in care, then nothing. "You do hate me," Maggie murmured in utter despair.

Maggie caught sight of her grandmother's carpetbag and pulled it close. She felt a lump in her throat as she thought of her grandmother sitting alone in the big Queen Anne house.

"Grandmother, I love you so. Please God, even if You can't forgive me, take care of Grandmother until I can get back to Topeka," Maggie murmured.

Her mind was overwhelmed with the events of the day. It had all happened so fast. Her father had been wise to handle the situation as he had, for she would have gone into hiding if she had she known of his plans.

In his own way, he had probably tried to tell her. Maggie's mind wandered back to an unopened stack of letters collecting dust in the attic back home. She had heard nothing from her father for two years after he left. When at last a letter had arrived, Maggie had refused to read it. Grandmother had been understanding, Maggie remembered, but she had also engaged her granddaughter in discussions about forgiveness and God's overall plan.

"Oh, Grandmother," Maggie sighed.

She opened the bag and removed its contents one by one. There were a dozen or more biscuits, and Maggie knew they'd be the lightest, finest soda biscuits ever made. Next she pulled out several pieces of fruit and a large chunk of cheese that her grandmother had lovingly wrapped in an embroidered tea towel. Maggie reached down deep and touched something quite familiar. She began to sob. It was her grandmother's Bible.

Maggie hugged the Bible to her chest and cried. Her pain grew more intense. She allowed the Bible to fall open. The final verse of the Old Testament loomed prophetically across the page: " 'And he shall turn the heart of the fathers to the children, and the heart of the children to their fathers, lest I come and smite the earth with a curse' " (Malachi 4:6).

"But this can't be right," Maggie said aloud, snapping the book shut. "Grandmother needs me, and I need her. My father hasn't turned his heart to me, and I certainly won't turn mine to him. Will You curse me without considering my side of the matter?"

Just then a knock sounded at the door, and Maggie began to tremble uncontrollably. Was it Garrett? What would she say?

Silently, Maggie placed the food in the carpetbag and set it on the floor. Then she eased down to the mattress, pulled her legs up under her, and feigned sleep. The knock sounded again, then the soft voice of the porter called her name. Finally, there was nothing.

Afraid to move, Maggie succumbed to the weariness that possessed her body and drifted into a fitful sleep. The day's events combined with the heat had been too much.

Maggie dreamed of a field of prairie flowers. Tall Kansas sunflowers waved majestically above the knee-high prairie grass. Bachelor buttons and sweet williams dotted the landscape with vivid purples and blues. She was running and running across the prairie until she could feel her legs ache from the strain. She pushed herself to continue until the pain in her legs became unbearable. Maggie felt herself falling in slow motion. Down she went to the velvety softness of new prairie grass.

Someone was calling her name, and when she opened her eyes, she met the bluest eyes she'd ever known. Garrett Lucas!

Maggie struggled to move away from Garrett, but it was no use. Her legs were badly cramped, and the pain she'd felt in her dream had become a very real sensation.

"Don't touch me!" Maggie winced in pain as she tried to move her legs.

"Stop fighting me. I'm not going to hurt you," Garrett said gently as he tried to help Maggie sit up.

"I don't want your help, and I don't want you here. Why are you here?" she suddenly questioned, forgetting her fear.

"We're in Florence. It's a supper stop. I've only come to wake you up and take you to supper," Garrett reasoned.

Maggie laughed nervously. "Supper? You think that I'm interested in eating? You waltz into my life, take me away from everything I love, tell me I have no choice — no say, and," she paused, drawing a deep breath to steady her nerves, "you top it off by telling me that you — you, Garrett Lucas — are to be my husband. And now you act as if nothing has happened and come to take me to supper?" Maggie tried to pull away from

Garrett but found herself pinned against the wall of her compartment.

"I told you to stop fighting me. I'm not going to hurt you. I have the highest respect for your father and for you," said Garrett in a hushed whisper. Maggie could barely hear him above the noise of her own ragged breathing.

Garrett's face was only a matter of inches from her own. Maggie swallowed hard and felt her face flush. She stopped fighting and matched Garrett's stare with one of her own.

Neither one said a word. Suddenly, Maggie knew her life would never be the same. By some means, her father and Garrett would have their way. What made it worse was that Garrett sensed this understanding in her.

Garrett moved his face closer, and Maggie closed her eyes, certain that he would kiss her. She'd never been kissed before, and part of her wondered what it would feel like.

When nothing happened, Maggie opened her eyes to find Garrett had pulled away. He looked at her with smug satisfaction, and Maggie wanted to disappear. How could he stir such intense feelings that her anger melted away, leaving her helpless to fight him?

"Shall we go to supper?" Garrett drawled, enjoying the upper hand. He helped Maggie to her feet and steadied her as she waited for the blood to return to her legs.

"I suppose I have no other choice," Maggie said soberly. "Lead me where you will, Mr. Lucas."

CHAPTER 5

Maggie went through the motions of eating dinner. She said very little, even though the food was some of the best she'd ever enjoyed. Maggie had never eaten at a Harvey House. She and her grandmother had always intended to do so but had never gotten to it.

Garrett had ordered the English-style baked veal pie for himself as well as Maggie. Accompanying the veal were fresh vegetables and a selection of salads, one of which was made with lobster brought in from the East.

Maggie wanted to show as little interest as possible, but her curiosity got the best of her once or twice. When the Harvey girl brought out dessert, Maggie nearly moaned.

"I don't know where I could put another bite," Maggie said to the young woman. "Just look at this piece of pie!"

Garrett smiled to himself, happy to see

Maggie talking, if only to the Harvey girl.

"It's a quarter slice, Ma'am. That's the way Mister Harvey says it's to be done. He doesn't want his customers leaving the Harvey House hungry." The girl curtsied.

"No chance of that," Garrett joined in good-naturedly. The Harvey girl smiled appreciatively at Garrett, and for some reason, Maggie felt angry.

"If you'll excuse me, Mr. Lucas," Maggie said, getting to her feet. "I will have this young woman show me where I can freshen up."

Garrett's eyes narrowed. They sent Maggie a silent warning, but she merely tossed Garrett a smile over her shoulder and followed the Harvey girl from the room.

"You'll find provisions to wash up at the end of the hall. The rest is out the back door," the Harvey girl pointed. "I've got to return to my station now."

Maggie lingered several minutes at the back door. It would be easy enough to slip from sight, but to where? If she left, Garrett would be right on her trail, and there would be no chance to escape before he found her.

She turned her attention to the pitcher of water on the alcove table. She poured a small amount into the bowl and took a fresh wash cloth from the stack beside the pitcher.

Dipping the cloth over and over, Maggie managed to wash away most of the day's grime. Taking a comb from her bag, Maggie tried to put her hair back in order. She'd lost several hairpins.

Convinced that she had done her best, Maggie started back down the hall. As she neared the entrance to the dining room, she noticed a large map of the state. The rail line was clearly outlined and included the many spurs that ran from the main line to a variety of small Kansas towns.

Maggie traced the route. There would be a variety of whistle stops in between, but Newton would offer her the best chance of getting home. A smile played on her lips. "We'll see just how smug Garrett Lucas is when he wakes up in western Kansas and I'm gone," Maggie whispered under her breath.

In the dining room, Garrett was finishing a cup of coffee. His relaxed appearance gave no hint of his inner turmoil. Four times, Garrett had checked on Maggie, making sure she hadn't disappeared. Now as she took her seat across from him once again, he was captivated by the beauty he saw. Although he'd accused her of being a child, it was increasingly clear she was a young woman.

"The train's been delayed," he told Maggie. "We can wait it out here or on board. What's your choice?"

Maggie said nothing, pretending to take sips of tea. Pushing the fine china cup back to its saucer, she forced herself to meet Garrett's eyes.

"It is of little consequence to me, Mr. Lucas. I leave the matter entirely up to you," she said icily. Each word had been carefully chosen and delivered.

"Very well. Let's return to the train." Garrett motioned toward the door. He left a generous tip of thirty cents and helped Maggie from her chair.

Maggie waited patiently while Garrett paid for the meal with money her father had provided. She felt angry at the thought of her father's scheming but said nothing as Garrett led her back to the train. Outside, the weather had turned chilly, and Maggie was glad she'd worn her heavy traveling suit.

Garrett walked slowly and made small talk about the town of Florence. Maggie feigned interest and even glanced north at the main part of town, but she breathed a sigh of relief when Garrett finally led her back to the train.

"You've been awfully quiet," Garrett drawled, making note of Maggie's sigh. "I don't suppose you'd give up this playacting and talk to me."

Maggie raised an eyebrow and lifted her face to meet Garrett's inquisitive stare. "I don't know what you want me to say, Mr. Lucas. I'm tired and confused, and as a spoiled and selfish child, I can't imagine having anything to say that could be of interest to you."

It was Garrett's turn to sigh. "Maggie, that's not true. First off, I wish you'd call me Garrett."

"First? What next?" Maggie questioned in a sarcastic tone.

"Frankly, I wish you'd sit a spell with me. It's early, and you'll have plenty of time to rest later." Garrett was as polite and considerate as Maggie had ever seen him.

"Very well — Garrett. I will sit with you," Maggie said, trying to put Garrett's mind at ease. It was important to make him believe she'd accepted her fate.

Garrett felt his chest tighten when Maggie said his name. He grinned broadly as he helped her board the train and led her down the aisle to the window seat.

For a moment, Garrett stood admiring Maggie's profile. The lanterns above the aisles threw a mysterious glow. In their gentle light, Maggie looked more a woman than her seventeen years.

Maggie grew uncomfortable under Garrett's detailed scrutiny. "What was it you wanted to discuss, Mr. Lu . . . , Garrett?" Maggie questioned, hoping he'd stop examining her face.

"Maggie, you don't need to be afraid of me," he said softly, taking the seat beside her.

"I'm not . . ." Her words trailed off. There was no sense in lying. "I guess it's just a natural reaction," she finally admitted.

"Of course," Garrett agreed. "I wouldn't expect anything else, but I want to put your mind at ease if I can."

Maggie wished she could freeze the moment in time. The muted light of the train, the star-filled sky beyond the windows, and Garrett Lucas looking at her in a way no other man had ever done.

Garrett closed his brown, calloused hand over her small, soft fingers. Maggie's breath caught in her throat. She tried to will herself to pull her hand away.

"I wish you wouldn't do that," she whispered without daring to look into Garrett's blue eyes.

"Is that the truth, Maggie?" Garrett inquired, daring her to face her feelings. He knew playing upon those feelings might jeopardize the progress that had been made, but human nature urged him on.

Maggie touched her free hand to her forehead. "I can't think clearly when you're close by."

Garrett laughed out loud, causing several of the train passengers to lift their eyes from newspapers and embroidery work. Maggie was grateful their nosey train companion had departed. Garrett gave Maggie's hand a squeeze.

"That's a good sign, Magdelena, *mi querida,*" he murmured, so low that Maggie could barely make out the words.

"What does that mean?" she questioned, not certain she wanted an answer.

"I'll tell you later," Garrett grinned. "I don't think you could appreciate it right now."

Maggie spoke out boldly. "A term of endearment, no doubt." The warmth of Garrett's hand seemed to radiate up her arm.

"Would you hate that so very much?" he inquired.

Maggie didn't trust herself to answer. She lowered her face as she felt blood rush to her cheeks.

"I'm sorry," Garrett said. "I shouldn't

66

have pressured you with something so intimate."

"No," Maggie whispered. "You shouldn't have." Silence fell like a heavy blanket between them. Maggie wished Garrett would remove his hand, but he didn't.

"Don't you have any questions about your father?" he asked. He hated to break the moment of intimacy by bringing up Jason's name.

"I suppose I am curious," Maggie said thoughtfully. She pulled her hand from Garrett's, pretending to loosen the lace collar at her neck. What she said was the truth, and it couldn't hurt to listen.

"Good. What would you like to know first?" Garrett questioned her as easily as if they'd been lifelong chums. This feeling of familiarity bothered Maggie.

"Start anywhere. I don't know much at all. Grandmother used to share bits and pieces with me, but she knew how uncomfortable it made me," Maggie replied absentmindedly.

"Why, Maggie? Why did it make you uncomfortable to hear about your father?" Garrett pried, hoping Maggie would answer truthfully.

"Because he'd hurt me so badly," Maggie blurted out. She couldn't help the tears that formed in her eyes. She turned her face to the window, but Garrett reached across, compelling her to face him.

"Sometimes it's necessary to open up a wound, to clean it out and let it heal. Life's like that too, Maggie," he said softly.

Maggie wiped a single tear away as it slid down her cheek. "Some wounds never heal, Garrett."

"They can with God's help. 'My heart is sore pained within me: and the terrors of death are fallen upon me.' That's from Psalms," Garrett offered.

"You know the Bible?" Maggie questioned in disbelief.

"Not as well as I'd like to, but I suppose more than some. I found religion a way of life when I was young. But it wasn't until after I lost my parents that I learned what a relationship with Jesus Christ was about," Garrett answered.

"I didn't know your parents were dead. What happened to them?" Maggie questioned, steering the conversation away from the issue of salvation.

"Their wagon overturned on a mountain road. They were hauling goods back from Santa Fe and never came home. I was twelve at the time."

68

"How awful," Maggie gasped. "What did you do?"

"I did the only thing I could do," Garrett shrugged. "I mourned their passing and was packed off to Denver to live with an aging aunt."

"You had no other family?" Maggie was suddenly quite interested.

"None. My mother's sister was quite a bit older. She was the only living relative I had in the world. Life out West isn't easy on people," Garrett reflected. "My aunt died two years later, and I took off on my own."

"Where did you meet my father?"

"I'd wandered down to Santa Fe," Garrett said, smiling sadly. "I was nearing my fifteenth birthday and feeling pretty sorry for myself. Here I was, a young man alone in the world. I was just existing, not really living. I felt God had deserted me. That's when your father came on the scene.

"I was sweeping out a livery stable for a man in Santa Fe. He paid me twenty cents a week and let me sleep in the loft. It wasn't much, and I was getting pretty tired of it. My parents and aunt had left me some money, but I couldn't touch it until I turned twenty-one. Since my fifteenth birthday was coming up, I figured I'd take my week's wages and blow it at the saloon.

"I'd never been to a saloon, but I guzzled down as much rotgut as I could buy. I sat there nursing the last few drops in my glass, when it hit my head and stomach at the same time. I made a mad dash for the back door and the alley. That's where I met your pa."

"My father?" Maggie asked surprised.

"He happened to be walking down the alley just then. Most nights he'd walk for hours by himself. You have to remember, he'd just come to this territory. He'd lost your mother and baby son and had had to leave behind a baby daughter. If I had been five minutes later to the alley, I'd have missed him all together."

"What happened?"

"I thought I was dying, but your father helped me, and when it was all over, we shared our troubles. Your father offered me the use of his hotel room, and we fast became friends."

"My father was depressed because of Mother's death, wasn't he?" Maggie asked, picking at imaginary lint on her skirt.

"Not really. Jason, your father that is, said he believed his wife was safely in heaven with your brother. He showed me where the Bible said there'd be no sorrow in heaven, so he knew she was happy. What he couldn't

70

abide was his need to separate his life from yours."

"Me? I was the reason he was so un-happy?" Maggie wanted to change the subject, yet in her heart she wanted to understand the years that had separated her from her father.

"He told me all he wanted to do was work so hard he could go to sleep without seeing your face. He told me how you'd stood at the gate, tears streaming down your face, calling for him over and over," Garrett paused, knowing Maggie was filled with the pain of this memory. He reached his arm around her shoulder and pulled her close.

Maggie allowed Garrett to hold her. She no longer hated her father for leaving her. What else could he have done? She had deserved to be left behind.

After a few minutes, Maggie composed herself and pulled away from the sanctuary of Garrett's strong arms.

"He just kept walking. He never looked back," Maggie began. "I ran the length of the fence calling him. I knew he blamed me for my mother's death. I needed so much to know he still loved me, but he said noth-ing."

"He couldn't, Maggie. Not and still walk away, and if he'd stayed, he knew he'd be

71

forever lost in his remorse and sorrow. It couldn't have been an easy decision," Garrett answered gently. "I can just see you as a little girl, standing there waiting for him by the gate, day after day."

"How did you know?" Maggie's surprised expression matched her tone.

"Your father told me, and I would imagine your grandmother told him. Maybe she thought it'd make him come home. Maybe she thought it would turn him around."

"But it didn't," Maggie said sadly.

"No, it didn't, but there is another reason your father sent for you rather than traveling to Topeka himself," Garrett said in a way that demanded her attention.

"What?" Maggie questioned.

"If you'll recall, your grandmother mentioned your father hasn't been well."

"Yes," Maggie murmured.

"Your father always intended to make things right. He thought if he gave you enough time, you'd outgrow your hatred. But now he doesn't have that luxury."

"Why not?" Maggie asked.

"Because he's dying, Maggie."

"That isn't possible! He's not an old man, and he has plenty of money for doctors and medicine. He can't be dying," Maggie stated in disbelief.

Garrett's eyes softened. "All the money in the world can't buy you a new heart. Jason's heart has worn itself out, and there's no way to make it right again. He's aged rapidly, lost a great deal of weight, and spends most of his days in bed."

Maggie let the news soak in. "How, how long . . ." Maggie couldn't ask the question.

"How long does he have?" Garrett filled in the words.

Maggie nodded.

"Only God knows for sure."

Maggie felt more tired than she'd ever been before. She could no longer deal with her painful past.

"Garrett, I believe I'd like to retire. I'm completely spent."

"I understand. Let me walk you to your sleeper." Garrett stood and offered Maggie his hand. For a moment she hesitated, but her heart reasoned away any objections. She placed her hand in Garrett's and allowed him to lead her down the train aisle.

The lantern in Maggie's sleeping compartment made the room look warm and inviting. She paused in the doorway.

"Good night, Garrett," she said. She tried to think of something else to say, but the intensity of Garrett's stare banished rational thought. Maggie could feel her heart beating in her throat. Garrett was too close, and his hand was still firmly around her arm.

When he leaned down and gently pressed his lips on hers, Maggie went limp. She'd never been kissed by anyone on the lips, until now.

The kiss lasted a heartbeat, but to Maggie it seemed like a lifetime. When Garrett raised his head to speak, Maggie kept her eyes lowered. "Good night," he said before retreating down the narrow train aisle.

CHAPTER 6

At midnight, the train entered Newton, Kansas. Maggie was jerked awake by raucous laughter and drunken singing. As she struggled to sit up, she remembered Garrett's kiss.

"I've got to get away from here," she said in a hushed whisper. The sound of breaking glass outside drew her attention, and she peeked out from behind the window shade. The depot's large white letters read, "Newton."

Surely, Garrett's asleep at this hour, Maggie thought. *I should leave now.* The girl rushed to find her clothes. She reached into the inner pocket of her jacket and found her money still safe.

The lantern burned very low, and Maggie hurried to the mirror and did her best to pull her hair back. She tied it with the ribbon that had held her lace collar at the neck of her blouse. "It'll have to do," she conceded, not totally satisfied with the results.

Maggie pulled her coat on quietly and grabbed the carpetbag. Gently she edged the door of her sleeping compartment open and checked the hallway for any sign of Garrett. There was none.

As quickly as she could, Maggie maneuvered through the shadowy corridors of the train car. At last she was rewarded with the exit door.

"Well, Miss, if you're getting off here, I'd suggest you hurry. Train's pulling out directly," the conductor told her in his disinterested manner. Maggie prayed that he wouldn't question Garrett's whereabouts.

"Thank you, I will," Maggie replied. "Can you tell me where the nearest hotel is?"

"That whitewashed clapboard over there," the conductor said, eyeing his watch. "Sorry, Ma'am. We're pulling out. Are you staying?"

"Yes," Maggie managed to say. She took a last look at the train. The laughter had died down, and there was just the muffled noise of several other passengers walking away from the railroad station. The conductor returned the steps to the platform of the train and waved his brass lantern to signal the engineer.

As the train groaned and jerked down the

tracks, Maggie thought of Garrett. She was almost sorry she'd outfoxed him. She chuckled to herself as she walked toward the hotel.

Maggie found sleeping quarters with only moderate difficulty. As tired as she felt, she would have gladly slept in the barn. The manager had given her a candle, and Maggie didn't bother to inspect the room other than to locate the bed.

She undressed and, with a quick breath, blew out the candle and settled into bed. Maggie thought about all the things Garrett had told her. A part of her wished she could break down the barriers between her father and herself, but Maggie was certain he would never forgive her. Loneliness filled her as she again saw herself as a child. She struggled to remember something, but it passed away quickly in the cloudiness of sleep.

Several hours later, Maggie woke with a start. She couldn't remember where she was. The sun was just starting to shine through the lace curtains of her hotel room window.

Maggie swung her legs over the side of the bed, newly aware of her surroundings. The room wasn't much to look at, but it was clean and safe. The girl shivered from the cold wooden floor as she crossed to the window.

Careful not to reveal that she was dressed only in her camisole and petticoat, Maggie pulled back the curtain. Most of Newton still slept, and she wondered what time it was.

It must be early, she thought to herself. Realizing she was hungry, Maggie placed the carpetbag on the bed and pulled out a soda biscuit. As she began to eat, she remembered the evening before when she'd dined with Garrett in Florence. The heady aroma of the Harvey House food lingered in her mind, making her biscuit seem inadequate.

She also remembered the intimate conversation, Garrett's touch, and their kiss. Maggie shook her head as if to dispel the memory, but it was no use. Dancing blue eyes and a gentle smile were all she could remember. That and the fact that she was supposed to become Garrett Lucas's wife.

Within an hour, Maggie was dressed. Her traveling suit was hopelessly wrinkled, but there was no use worrying about it. She took the carpetbag and headed downstairs.

"Morning, Miss." The same man who'd given her entrance the night before was greeting her as though he'd woken from an undisturbed night. Maggie couldn't help but smile.

"Good morning," she answered politely. Just then, half a dozen children came running through the lobby. They were laughing and playing tag.

"Now children," the man began. "You know the rules about running inside. Go on out if you're going to run." The children stopped long enough to acknowledge their father, and then rushed through the hotel door out onto the street.

"Now, Miss, what can I do for you?" he asked, turning his attention back to Maggie.

"When will the next train for Topeka be through?"

"Well, that's hard to say. Usually, the train you were just on transfers its passengers at Great Bend. Then it comes on back and picks up eastbound passengers," the man told her.

"Usually?" Maggie held her breath.

"They've been having trouble with the Arkansas River. Rains are causing grief with the flood levels. If there's much more rain, the Arkansas is going to be out of its banks, then there won't be any trains through for a spell."

"If it doesn't flood," Maggie began in a

hopeful tone, "when will the train be back through?"

"This afternoon."

Maggie bit her lower lip as she thought. Garrett was bound to know she was gone by now. If not, it wouldn't be much longer before he found out. She couldn't risk staying in Newton long enough for Garrett to return on the afternoon train.

"What about a horse? Where could I buy or rent a horse?" Maggie questioned innocently.

"You could check at the livery stable, but I wouldn't get my hopes up. Horses are hard to come by out here. You won't find too many people willing to rid themselves of one. Besides," the man answered, noticing Maggie's attire, "you aren't really dressed for riding."

Maggie tried to smile, but her mind was in a frenzy. If she couldn't get out of Newton within hours, Garrett would find her.

"What about the stage? Will there be a stagecoach or freighters leaving for Topeka today?" Maggie knew she was appearing desperate.

"I don't know what's chasing you, little lady, but the answer is no. Stage isn't due through here for another day," the proprietor said sympathetically. "I'd check with the livery stable first, but I'd say if you're going to leave Newton today, it'll be on foot."

Maggie nodded and thanked the man. She walked to the livery stable, where the livery owner told her there hadn't been a horse available for sale since February.

"Where you want to go, little lady?" a foul-smelling man asked Maggie.

"I'd rather not discuss it," Maggie said, growing increasingly uncomfortable as the man's friends joined him.

"She ain't your type, Jake," one of the man's filthy friends offered. "You're more my type, now ain't you?" The other men laughed and ribbed each other with their elbows.

"You saddle tramps git out. You hear me? Now git!" the livery owner bellowed. When the men begrudgingly walked away, Maggie turned to thank the man.

"I appreciate your help. I don't suppose there's any hope of someone hauling freight out this morning?"

"Nope, I'd know if there was. As far as I know, you're stuck here at least until tomorrow, probably more like next Friday. I don't think the train will get past the Arkansas River crossing."

A discouraged Maggie walked to the Harvey House and sat down for a hot breakfast. Her money was going fast, but if she did have to walk out as the hotel manager had mentioned, she would need proper nourishment.

While eating breakfast, Maggie learned the train she'd been on the night before had already turned back in the direction of Newton. The Harvey girl informed her they expected the train for the lunch meal.

Maggie wondered what she should do. She could try to hide out in Newton or get on the train after Garrett got off. She toyed with several ideas while absentmindedly stuffing food in her mouth. She was surprised to find herself nearly finished with her meal when the Harvey girl appeared at her table to see if she needed anything else.

By eight o'clock, Maggie had decided to walk to Florence. The town was a main hub for the stage, and freight was being hauled out every day. Maggie didn't know how long it would take to walk the thirty miles to Florence, but putting space between Garrett and herself was the only thing that mattered.

After paying for her breakfast, Maggie got directions to the general store and went in search of supplies.

A cheery bell rang on the door of the store

as Maggie entered. She was greeted by an elderly woman who eyed every stranger suspiciously.

"Where did you come from?" the woman questioned rudely.

"I'm from Topeka," Maggie answered, hoping her honesty would quell the woman's curiosity.

"Topeka? You came here from Topeka? When?"

"I came in last night, and now I'm getting ready to leave. I have a few things I need, and if you don't mind, I need to hurry," Maggie retorted rather harshly.

"You running from the law, Girl?" the woman continued to pry.

"Absolutely not!" Maggie exclaimed.

Quickly, Maggie located the things she needed for the walk. She was grateful she'd had the sense to wear walking shoes. She located a canteen and some dried fruit and placed them on the counter.

"I figure you must be planning on walking somewhere. I'd be mindful of the weather if I was you," the older woman said, seeming to soften a bit. "My big toe has been aching all night from the chill in the air. I figure a powerful storm is brewing, and we'll be due for rain tonight." Maggie nodded and paid the woman.

"You aren't going to walk far in that outfit are you?" the woman asked, smoothing back a strand of gray hair.

"It'll take me as far as I need to go," Maggie replied and walked out of the store.

Maggie knew following the train tracks would be the wisest thing to do. She also knew it would be the first place Garrett would look for her. She walked several yards before deciding to parallel the tracks as best she could without being seen. The prairie stretched out endlessly before her. Only an occasional stand of trees broke the monotony.

Remembering the old woman's warning, Maggie looked to the skies. Clouds were building to the west. Probably the same storm that had flooded the Arkansas River, Maggie surmised.

For a moment, she thought better of her decision to walk to Florence. She turned to survey Newton once again. Surely, it couldn't be that hard to find a hiding place.

She looked skyward again, and her mind turned to thoughts of God. Where was He in all this? Maggie couldn't help but wonder what God would want her to do. She'd spent so much of her life ignoring God's direction that now she felt ridiculous for her concern.

84

But maybe God wanted to use something in this to help her find her way. A place where Maggie could finally belong. She sighed. Why would God care about her? After all, she'd done nothing but turn her back on Him. No, Maggie decided, God certainly wouldn't listen to her now.

Calling upon every ounce of courage she possessed, Maggie moved north, away from the tracks. She knew she'd be able to see the telegraph wires from quite a distance, and the added space gave her a slight feeling of security. When Maggie felt confident she was far enough away from the tracks to be hidden by the tall prairie grass, she turned east. Determined to reach Florence as soon as possible, Maggie quickened her steps.

"Soon I'll be back where I belong," Maggie said aloud, trying desperately to bolster her sagging spirits. But in truth, Maggie wasn't sure where she belonged.

CHAPTER 7

By ten o'clock, Maggie knew leaving Newton had been a mistake. Her feet hurt and
her back ached. Sitting down, Maggie took
off her shoes and surveyed the terrain
around her. It was pretty enough, she
thought as she rubbed her blistered feet.
The fields were covered with tall, thick
prairie grass. In the distance, rolling hills
were covered with soft greens and purples.

Returning her shoes to her feet, Maggie
stood and brushed the grass from her skirt.
If only it were as easy to brush off the
emptiness that filled her heart!

The air felt heavy and sticky. The farther
Maggie walked, the more desperate she felt.

"But I had to leave," she reasoned aloud.
"I couldn't go on with him — with Garrett." Just saying his name reminded her of
the tender way he'd kissed her.

Growing up in Topeka, Maggie had
avoided both boys her own age and older

men who found her prime wife material. It was the age of the mail-order bride, and Maggie couldn't help but laugh out loud as she remembered one particular encounter. Harley T. Smythe, a local bride broker, had come unannounced to the Intissar home.

Maggie could still remember the stunned look on her grandmother's face as Mr. Smythe had explained his intentions of arranging a marriage for the older woman. Sophia had listened patiently, but not without discomfort. When at last Mr. Smythe took a breath, Sophia had interrupted and led him back to the front door.

"Mr. Smythe," Sophia had stated as she fairly pushed him through the portal. "I have no intention of remarrying." With that she closed the door in Harley T. Smythe's astonished face and let out a laugh matching Maggie's.

Maggie felt tears in her eyes. "I love you so much, Grandmother. You were always there for me, and you always made me happy." Maggie continued talking as if her grandmother walked beside her. Somehow it made the miles pass more quickly.

She had walked some distance when the grasslands started giving way to rockier scenery. The rocks were a nuisance, but there was no avoiding them.

Soon, Maggie came to another obstacle. A wide ravine, apparently a dry wash or creek bed, cut deep into the ground. Maggie considered her plight, but within seconds her mind was made up for her. The sound of riders caught her attention.

"Garrett!" The name caught in her throat. Three mounted horses were kicking up a fury of dust in the direction Maggie had just come from.

Without thinking, Maggie started down the edge of the ravine. The rocky gravel gave way, causing her to slide halfway into the small canyon. The ravine was deep and ran for miles either way, with small caves and inlets hidden in the rock walls. As she reached the bottom, Maggie hurried in the direction of the railroad tracks.

She kept straining to hear the sound of hooves. She knew the men must have seen her, and she began to run, tripping over larger rocks. She heard rumbling in the distance. The sky had grown dark. Her side began to hurt and her legs were cramping, but Maggie knew she had to continue running.

The ravine grew deeper and began twisting and turning. Maggie could see where the railroad trestle crossed the ravine. If she could make it to the trestle, she might find a place to hide. She hiked her skirts up higher and put all her strength into running. As she approached the trestle, her eyes darted back and forth. No sanctuary revealed itself.

Quickly, Maggie scurried under the trestle and continued down the ravine. Rain started to pour, and Maggie grew desperate as she heard a horse's whinny. The riders were very close.

" 'Deliver me in Thy righteousness, and cause me to escape: incline Thine ear unto me, and save me.' " She murmured the Psalm, surprised that she had remembered it. She thought about praying, but changed her mind. She never could abide the attitude of calling on God when one was in trouble, only to go one's own way when things went well.

Just when Maggie found it impossible to force herself any farther, an opening in the ravine wall revealed itself. It was scarcely more than a two-foot-wide indention, but Maggie could hug her rain-drenched body against the rock and avoid being seen by the riders above her.

A flash of lightning startled the girl, and she bit her lip to keep from crying out in surprise. The boom of thunder so soon after the lightning let her know the worst of the storm was nearly upon them. The wind picked up, muffling the riders' voices.

"I don't see her, Jake," one of the men called out. "Let's go back to town and out of this mess."

Maggie tensed. It wasn't Garrett after all but the ruffians from the livery stable in Newton. Remembering the look in Jake's eyes caused her to freeze in fear.

"I guess you're right. I'm pert near soaked to the bone already."

Maggie recognized Jake's grizzly voice. Another flash of lightning caused Maggie to jump. Overhead, the horses snorted and stamped.

"Come on. Let's git," Jake called to his companions. "Another day, little lady," he yelled in the direction of the ravine. Maggie shivered at the thought.

The men rode away, but with the storm growing stronger, Maggie stayed against the ravine wall. Thunder continued to boom out answers to lightning, and the sky grew even darker. Maggie noticed water collecting in the ravine bottom.

After another ten minutes, the lightning had lessened but not the rain. The water was nearly to Maggie's ankles, and it continued to rise.

I've got to get out of here, Maggie thought.

She began to wade toward the railroad bridge. The weight of her water-drenched skirts threatened to drag her down, but she held her skirts up above her knees and kept wading. She got to the trestle, thankful that the skies had lightened a little.

Maggie rested against one trestle support after another until she'd worked her way out of the ravine. At the top, she rested under the bridge and considered what to do next. The water had risen even higher and resembled a small creek.

Suddenly, Maggie became aware of what a sheltered life she'd led. Someone had always been close at hand to help her out of trouble. While she'd learned many social graces and home skills, she was just as Garrett had said: a spoiled and selfish child.

When the rain let up, Maggie continued her journey toward Florence. The sky was overcast, but the sun was beginning to heat things up. Maggie felt sticky and uncomfortable in her clothes.

The clouds began to build again, and huge thunderheads were lining the horizon to the west. Maggie recognized signs of another storm. She picked up her pace, but because of her blisters, she just as quickly slowed down again.

Tears welled in Maggie's eyes. All she

wanted to do was go home, care for her Grandmother Intissar, and be happy. Why would God begrudge her that? But Maggie already knew the answer. God was not making war on her. She was making war on God.

Refusing to deal with the issue of God and her need for Him, Maggie concentrated on each step. "I'm one step closer to Topeka. I'm that much closer to home," she murmured as the soggy ground mushed up around her feet.

The sky grew darker as the squall line neared. Maggie felt even more vulnerable than before. Part of her wanted to sit down on the waterlogged ground and cry, but she knew that she had to find shelter.

Maggie could see very little that constituted a safe haven. Ahead to the north was a small stand of trees. They weren't likely to offer much protection, but perhaps they would buffer the wind. As Maggie pushed forward, she remembered her grandmother's warning about trees and lightning. She knew she was being foolish, but the alternative of open prairie seemed far less appealing.

Maggie barely reached the trees when the first huge raindrops began to fall. The sky had taken on a greenish hue, a sure sign of hail.

The trees offered little cover. The brush around them was laden with dead leaves, grass, and twigs. Maggie chose a spot surrounded on three sides by young trees, hoping that if lightning proved to be a problem, it would strike taller, older trees.

The wind picked up and chilled Maggie to the bone. Rain pelted her from every direction. Maggie hid her face in the carpetbag, refusing to watch the violence around her.

After what seemed hours, the storm played itself out, leaving colder temperatures behind. Maggie began to walk, no longer able to bear the pain and cold of sitting crouched against the trees.

There was little hope of reaching Florence before night, and Maggie began to wonder how she would endure a night on the prairie. If she continued walking after dark, there would be no way of knowing where she was. But if she stopped, she'd have to sleep out in the open.

Maggie walked on in the fading light. Every part of her body was saturated from the rain, and the weight of her clothing was slowing her pace to a near crawl. Finally, as the last bit of light slipped over the horizon,

Maggie dropped to her knees in the soggy prairie grass.

The prairie sky filled with stars, and the moon darted in and out from behind clouds. Maggie huddled shivering on the ground below. Her senses were dulled from the cold, and her mind was groggy with sleep. The last thing she remembered was the distant howl of a coyote.

The next morning dawned bright and clear, but the wind was still cold. Typical of Kansas weather, summer didn't guarantee warmth.

Maggie pulled herself to a sitting position and waited for her head to stop spinning. When the dizziness refused to subside, she began to panic. She shook her head and felt blinding pain.

Slowly, she got to her feet and tried to get her bearings. There was no sign of the railroad or the telegraph poles. There was nothing to do but walk in the direction of the rising sun. At least that would put her in an eastward direction.

Minutes worked into hours, and Maggie still had no indication that she was where she ought to be. She strained her eyes to catch some sign of life but saw nothing except hills and rocky fields.

When the sun was nearly overhead, Maggie stopped and ate some of the food from her carpetbag. It satisfied her hunger but did nothing to clear her head. She rested on the grass for a moment, fighting dizziness. Mindful that precious time was escaping, Maggie summoned all her strength in order to push on.

She got on her hands and knees and tried to stand, but immediately fell back to the ground. She tried again and again, but it was no use. Finally, Maggie gave up and let her body slump to the ground.

"I give up God!" she cried to the heavens. "I give up. Whatever it is You want, I accept. I won't fight anymore. If marrying Garrett Lucas and living in the New Mexico Territory are best for me, then so be it. I will not defy Your will any longer. But, please, please help me now. Show me what to do, where to go! Please!"

Maggie was unable to keep her eyes open. She dreamed of warm fires and her grandmother's hot chocolate. She was vaguely aware of a dull ache in her head and chest, but she couldn't rally enough strength to figure out why she hurt so much.

When next she opened her eyes, the sun was just setting on the horizon. Or was it rising? Maggie tried to get some sense of the time of day, but her mind refused to

95

register anything but pain. She coughed until she nearly passed out. The intense cold made her shake violently.

At one point, Maggie opened her eyes and thought she saw people in the distance, but when she squeezed her eyes tight and opened them again, she realized it was just her imagination.

The sky grew dark and the ground grew colder than ever. Maggie's teeth began to chatter uncontrollably. She didn't hear the approaching sound of horse hooves, and she barely felt the hands that gently turned her over and helped her to sit. When she opened her eyes, she could only gasp one word before falling back against the offered support.

"Garrett."

Maggie saw tears in Garrett's eyes as he cradled her in his arms. They couldn't be real, she decided. Nor could the words she heard him saying.

"Maggie, my Maggie. What would I do if I lost you now? Please, God don't let her die!"

No. Those words were only her wishful imagination, Maggie decided as she drifted into sleep.

CHAPTER 8

It seemed only moments had passed since Maggie had last opened her eyes. But looking above, she was dumfounded to find mud, thatch, and sod hanging over thin poles. Where was she? Maggie struggled in vain to remember what had happened on the rain-drenched prairie.

Mindless of the pain in her chest, Maggie sat up and began coughing violently. A bearded Garrett Lucas rushed into the room to her side.

"Try to take a sip of water," he said, gently supporting her back while handing her a tin cup. Maggie did as he said and found her cough abated somewhat.

"What happened? Where are we?" Maggie whispered hoarsely. She was puzzled that Garrett wore a beard and his attire had so drastically changed since last she'd seen him on the train.

Garrett went to the small cook stove and

returned with the cup.

"Drink this," he instructed.

Maggie took the cup and looked inside. It held a thick black syrup. "What is it?" she questioned skeptically.

"It's medicine to clear out your lungs," Garrett replied, concern hanging thick in his voice.

"Your stomach too, I'd venture to say," Maggie said, trying to lighten his mood.

Garrett laughed at Maggie's words. It was so good to hear her speak, even if to question his actions.

"I'm glad I amuse you, but what in the world has happened? I remember walking out of Newton, and the terrible storms, but after that . . ." Maggie paused trying her best to remember.

"Drink first, and then we'll talk," Garrett said, pointing to the cup. Maggie screwed up her face at the thought of drinking the medicine but did as Garrett instructed. The blend wasn't so bad. Maggie finished it and held the empty cup up as proof.

Garrett set the cup aside and pulled up a crude wooden chair. "Now, I believe we have some things to discuss." His dark brown hair was a bit wild, and the beard made him look older.

Maggie was captivated by the way Garrett

looked, but she refused to acknowledge even the slightest admiration. She waited for Garrett to continue.

"I don't know what in the world you were thinking, getting off a train in the middle of the night," Garrett tried unsuccessfully to sound stern. When he looked at Maggie, even in her sickly state, she was all he'd ever wanted. She was beautiful, intelligent, hardworking, and resourceful — although, he would have to teach her a bit more about that last quality.

"I wanted to go home to my grandmother," Maggie offered lamely.

Garrett ignored her remark. "I went to let you know the train was turning back because of the flood waters. I had the porter open your door when you didn't answer, and —" His voice caught. "I felt like dying inside when I saw you were gone."

"Father would have been quite miffed with you, eh?" Maggie teased, still refusing to acknowledge the seriousness of the situation.

"Don't you know how close you came to dying?" Garrett's face contorted painfully.

"I suppose very close."

"You suppose that, do you? Well, if I hadn't come riding up when I did, you wouldn't have lived another hour. You were drenched to the bone and nearly unconscious. I was lucky enough to locate a doctor. He and his wife agreed to let us stay here in their dugout."

"So, this is a dugout?" Maggie murmured while looking around the small room. Everything seemed to touch. What little furniture she could see was poorly put together, not at all what one would expect a doctor to have. The dugout had been dug by hand, some six or eight feet into the earth. The roof rose above the prairie only two or three feet.

"Yes, this is a dugout. But that isn't the issue. Maggie, please promise me you won't run away again. I can't imagine returning to your father or grandmother and explaining that you got yourself killed."

Maggie could sense the genuine concern in Garrett's voice. *Why did he care so much? He hardly knew her.*

"I'm sorry, Garrett. I shouldn't have run, but I was scared. I kept thinking about never seeing Grandmother again. Then I thought about having to face my father and his condemnation. All that along with what it would be like to . . ." Her words faded as she nearly mentioned the idea of becoming Garrett's wife. Embarrassed, Maggie lowered her face.

"I put a great deal of pressure on you," Garrett apologized. "I'm sorry for that. Back in New Mexico, the plan seemed so right."

"I guess sometimes we only seek our own way," Maggie said softly. "I don't think I've ever done as much praying as I have in the last few hours. Not that I really expected God to listen to me."

"Last few hours? How long do you think we've been here, Maggie?"

"I was just going to ask you that."

"Five days," Garrett replied dryly.

"Five?"

"That's right." Garrett leaned back against the chair. "Five days of wondering and waiting. Praying that you'd live but feeling so helpless. That's part of what I wanted to talk to you about."

"I can't believe it's been that long. It seems like just hours ago I was bartering with God for my rescue, and here you are."

"Oh, Maggie. I wish it was that simple. I found you, brought you here, and waited. Doc said he'd done all he could. We took turns watching over you. I told God if He would make you well, I'd never force you to marry me." There. He'd finally said the words.

Maggie burst out laughing, and with the

laughter came the cough again.

"Maybe we should wait. Maybe you aren't up to this," Garrett hastily suggested, concerned that she was becoming hysterical.

"No, pl . . . please," Maggie sputtered the words, trying to contain her cough. "Don't take offense. I'm only laughing because I made a similar deal with God myself. I told him I'd do whatever He wanted me to, even if that meant marrying you and living with Father. I said if God would rescue me, I'd stop fighting Him."

"I see," Garrett said thoughtfully, realizing Maggie had said nothing of a commitment to Jesus. "Seems we've both been bartering with God."

"Grandmother would chastise me," Maggie admitted. "She used to say, 'Never offer God anything you aren't ready, willing, and able to give.' "

"And now, Maggie." Garrett's voice was barely audible, "are you ready, willing, and able to follow God's direction for your life?"

"What about you, Garrett Lucas?" Maggie avoided the question.

"It seems to me, God saved us both in spite of ourselves. I don't think we thought too clearly. I'd hate to be rash with any decision, but I did promise God I'd leave you be."

Maggie tried not to show her disappointment. Part of her was starting to like the idea of becoming Mrs. Garrett Lucas.

"I promised God I would do anything, even live with my father and become your wife. I can't break a vow to God," Maggie answered honestly.

"I'd say there's something important to learn from this. We need to seek God's will over our own. He'll guide us, but He can't if we're always trying to lead," Garrett reflected.

"I believe that's true. I guess I'm ready to try harder at trusting Him," Maggie added.

"Even with your life?"

Maggie lowered her eyes and fingered the sheets nervously. "I don't know. I don't want to make that kind of decision lightly, and I don't want to make it simply because I'm scared. I want it to mean more than that."

Garrett nodded. "I wouldn't presume to rush you. You'll make the right choice when God's timing is complete."

"Thank you for understanding," Maggie whispered. "I appreciate that more than you'll ever know."

"I wonder, Maggie," Garrett mused, leaning toward her from the edge of his chair. "I wonder if we could start over."

"Start over? What do you mean?"

"I'd like to be your friend, even if I never become your husband. Although," Garrett added with a wry smile, "I'd like to be that too."

Maggie blushed.

"I believe," she replied after a thoughtful moment, "we could be friends. I will be your friend and I will go to my father's ranch willingly. On that I give you my word."

Garrett gently lifted Maggie's chin. He studied her delicate cheekbones and dainty lips. When he looked into Maggie's eyes, he found a sincerity he hadn't dared to hope for.

"I know it will please your father, and if it means much," Garrett added, "it pleases me."

"Garrett, please don't rush me about my father. I still feel uncomfortable about this whole thing. I won't lie and tell you otherwise. I feel trapped, but I know that going to him is the right thing." Maggie tried to clear the hoarseness in her voice. "I can't pretend I feel anything but pain about the past and my father."

"I understand. I just love Jason so much.

He's been like a father to me." Garrett immediately regretted the words.

"I wish he'd been a father to me," Maggie breathed.

"I wish he could have too. Selfishly, I'm glad he left Topeka. I'd be a far worse man if I'd never met him. But because I care for you, I'm sorry he had to leave you."

He cared for her. Maggie warmed at the thought. Refusing to get carried away, Maggie pushed the feeling aside.

"There are a great many things I wish I could change," she finally said, looking up at the sod roof. "But wishing doesn't make it so. It doesn't bring people back to life, or give you a place to belong."

"Maggie, you'll always have a place to belong. You belong to God, but you just don't know it yet. You belong with your father, but you can't get past the mistakes. And," Garrett sighed, "I'd like to think you belong with me."

Maggie offered a gentle smile. "All I can do is try," she replied. "But it's going to take time, and I'll need your understanding."

"I promise to help in whatever way I can." Garrett whispered the words although he wanted to shout in triumph. With God's help, he had broken through the wall of protection Maggie had built around herself. The foundation for friendship had been laid.

An hour later, a white-haired woman came bustling through the door and down the dirt stairs of the dugout. She huffed as she struggled to carry in a basket of vegetables.

"Well, look who's awake," she said, spying Maggie.

Garrett smiled broadly. "We've already had quite a lively conversation. I gave her some medicine and made her stay put."

"I must say, Child, you gave us quite a fright. Doc will be mighty happy to see you've pulled out of it," the woman remarked, stepping to Maggie's bedside.

"Maggie, this is Dottie. She's the doctor's wife," Garrett introduced. "She and Doc have allowed us the pleasure of staying here until you get well enough to travel."

"It's a pleasure to meet you," Maggie said sweetly. "It's so kind of you to let us stay here."

"Ain't nothing at all. I was glad for the company. Doc doesn't always make it home very early, and it gets mighty lonesome out here on the plains. I was glad to have you both, 'specially this one," Dottie nodded toward Garrett. "He's been a Godsend — brings me fresh water for the garden and totes and fetches just about anything else I need."

"If she'd waited, I would have carried in those vegetables too," Garrett added with an admonishing look.

"Weren't that heavy. Didn't see any reason to go bothering you." Dottie waved him off. "Now how about you, Missy. Hungry?"

"I think I am," Maggie replied, realizing she wanted something to eat.

"Good. I was just about to get us some lunch. Broth for you and stew and biscuits for us." The older woman pulled on a clean apron.

Maggie wrinkled her nose. She'd hoped for something more substantial. Nonetheless, she felt very fortunate and cared for. She pushed aside the nagging thought that God had watched over her.

Day after day flew by. As Maggie grew stronger, she spent more time contemplating her life. She also developed a real love for Dottie and Doc. The older man had infinite patience and entertained his patient with humorous stories from his practice.

Maggie enjoyed watching Doc and Dottie as they playfully bantered words. Doc teased Dottie as if she were a young schoolgirl, and Maggie noticed Dottie blushing on more than one occasion. *It must be wonder-*

ful to love each other so much after so many years of marriage, Maggie thought.

Eager to be up and around, Maggie talked Doc into letting her get out of bed at the end of the first week. As the end of the second week neared, she and Garrett began talking about the trip back to Newton.

"With the horse I bought in Newton, we can make it back to town in a matter of hours," Garrett began, as he and Maggie strolled along the outside of the dugout. The sky threatened rain any minute, and Garrett wouldn't allow them a longer walk. "Or Doc could drive us in his buckboard. I thought I could leave him the horse as partial payment for all he and Dottie have done. They don't have a good saddle horse."

Maggie remembered her unsuccessful search for a horse.

"How did you ever find a horse to buy in Newton?"

Garrett's eyes danced with amusement. "I take it you tried and failed?"

"Yes, as a matter of fact, but —" Maggie's words were lost in the rumble of thunder.

"I think we should get inside," Garrett suggested.

"I agree. I've been in one too many storms already," Maggie said, turning toward the dugout steps.

The storm roared across the prairie. The roof of the dugout leaked, and it swayed in the gusty winds. Maggie had to light the lamp twice because of the draft from the storm.

"We'll be lucky if there isn't hail," Garrett stated as he cracked open the door and looked out. "I'm glad Dottie went to town with Doc this morning."

"Do you think it will get much worse?" Maggie asked, paling at the thought.

"I don't know. The rain's letting up some, and the wind is dying down. Maybe the worst is past. I'm going to take a look," Garrett replied and opened the door. "You stay put."

Maggie watched Garrett's booted feet disappear up the stairs. Curious about what was happening, she followed him. He seemed intent on something to the south, and when Maggie made it to the top of the stairs, she found out why. She gasped as she caught sight of a large tornado heading toward them.

"I told you to stay down there!" Garrett yelled, pointing to the dugout.

"Dear God," Maggie breathed her prayer. "Deliver us."

The twister played out its energy on the open prairie, darting from side to side as if in some frenzied dance. Maggie could see bits of dirt and debris flying up in the air as the storm approached. The tornado was enormous, and its path still headed directly toward the dugout.

"Let's take cover," Garrett said.

"Where?" Maggie asked fearfully, running down the stairs in front of him. There were tears in her eyes.

Garrett took everything off the table and pushed it against the wall of the dugout.

"Here. Get under the table." He pulled the mattress and blankets off the bed.

"Take these," he said, thrusting the blankets at Maggie's huddled frame. He crawled under the table and pulled the mattress in with him, securing it around them to shield them from any debris.

"Give me those blankets," he instructed.

Maggie started to hand the blankets over when the roaring of the wind caught her attention. It had started as a dull, constant noise in the background. Now it sounded as if a train were nearly upon them. Maggie caught Garrett's expression and knew instinctively it was the tornado.

Garrett grabbed the blankets and pulled them over their heads. He wrapped his arms around Maggie as the door to the dugout burst open, and the roof began to give way.

Above the roar of the Kansas twister, Garrett began to pray. "Dear Father, protect us from the destruction of this storm and give us shelter in Your watchful care. We pray this in Jesus' name. Amen."

"Amen," Maggie murmured in agreement. Warmth washed over her and her fears abated even though the storm continued to roar. Was this the peace of God that her grandmother had tried so often to explain?

Suddenly, Maggie found it difficult to breathe. It was as if all the air was being sucked out of the room. Her ears popped from the pressure of the storm. But more than anything else, she felt Garrett's strong arms around her.

CHAPTER 9

The storm completely destroyed the roof of the dugout, but Maggie and Garrett escaped without a scratch. Maggie was amazed by the power of the storm, but even more, she wondered at the power of God to protect them from destruction.

When Doc and Dottie returned to the dugout, Garrett was already repairing the roof and Maggie was clearing debris.

"We were lucky," Doc said as he gave Garrett a hand with the long roof poles. "The twister didn't touch Newton."

"We were blessed here too," an exhausted Garrett answered. "The twister only skirted the edge of the dugout. The barn and smokehouse had some shingles blown off, but the rest of the farm is undamaged."

Maggie and Dottie carried handfuls of sod outside and stopped to appraise the situation.

"Could'a been a lot worse," Dottie said,

wiping sweat from her forehead.

"That's just what Garrett was saying, Dot," Doc replied as he secured his end of the support poles.

"I've been through some bad storms before, but usually it was from the comfort of a cellar," Maggie exclaimed, still amazed at the calm, unchanged land around them.

"Well, these dugouts work nearly as well," Doc exclaimed and took the sod and branches that Maggie still held. The four worked until nightfall. After a hearty supper of Dottie's fried potatoes and pork chops, everyone went to bed early.

Days later the dugout was back in order, and Dottie declared it better than ever. Maggie seemed to thrive on the physical work, and Doc declared her completely healed. With that announcement, Garrett determined he and Maggie should move on to Newton and catch the earliest westbound train.

Maggie was sorry to leave Doc and Dottie, but more than that, she was scared to be traveling alone once again with Garrett. It wasn't that his company was unpleasant. It was the pleasure she found in his companionship that worried Maggie. Her fear was clearly reflected in her eyes, and she flinched when Garrett took hold of her arm after he'd finished packing their meager possessions in the buckboard.

"It's going to be alright, Maggie," Garrett whispered as he helped her into the wagon. "Trust me."

Maggie met Garrett's eyes. Excitement surged through her as she realized that this man would one day be her husband. *Trust him?* Maggie questioned her heart. *Was that possible?*

Maggie roused from her thoughts as Garrett and Doc sat down on either side of her. She waved a bittersweet goodbye to Dottie, promising to write. But once the farm was out of sight, Maggie fell back into silence. She thought about the future and wondered about God.

Maybe her grandmother had been right. Maybe Maggie never felt like she belonged because she didn't. She didn't belong to God.

Maggie lost herself in the memory of things her grandmother had told her about salvation. Over many Sunday dinners, the older woman had gently shared the need for Jesus Christ and eternal life.

"One can't outrun or outgrow one's need for Jesus, Maggie," Sophia had reminded her granddaughter. "Oh, people try. They find ways to compensate for the loss of God in their life."

"Such as?" Maggie had questioned.

"Well, look at Lillie." Sophia had referred to Maggie's friend. "There is no need for God in Lillie's life, at least as far as she is concerned. Her money brings everything she thinks she needs."

"Don't be hard on Lillie. She's very precious to me," Maggie had argued with her grandmother.

"Exactly. If you knew Lillie was in danger — the kind of danger that could take her life — and you could show her how to be saved from that perilous end, would you save her?" Maggie remembered the question as if it had been yesterday.

"Of course, Grandmother, you know I'd give my life for Lillie," Maggie had replied, knowing where the conversation was leading.

"Well, Maggie, Jesus has already given His life for Lillie and for you. You are both in risk of an eternal danger that I can never save you from. I can help you to see the need, but only God can deal with your heart, and only Jesus can save you from death."

Maggie chilled at the memory of her grandmother's words. She rubbed her temples. If only there weren't so many things to consider.

Garrett arranged for rooms at the Harvey House in Newton, and Maggie was grateful to find bathing accommodations that didn't require a metal wash pan. She lingered for a long time in the hot water.

"I do believe in God," Maggie reasoned with herself in the tub. "I just don't know about trusting Him with everything. Surely God expects me to take care of myself, especially when I get myself into trouble through carelessness." Just then a flash of pigtails, a bedroom window, and her mother's smile came to mind. Despite her best efforts, Maggie couldn't focus the memory. *What was haunting her?*

After warming the water in the tub twice, Maggie pulled a soft fluffy towel around her and prepared for dinner. She went to a small wardrobe and pulled out a pale blue silk gown, lavishly trimmed with Irish lace and satin ribbons.

Maggie pulled the dress over her head and gently smoothed it out. The Harvey House laundress had done a good job of removing most of the wrinkles. Maggie fastened the tiny buttons up the back of the gown, struggling to secure the last few.

She stood back to survey herself in the mirror, fluffing the slight fullness of the sleeves. Satisfied, Maggie sat down to the task of putting her hair in order. After another fifteen minutes, she was finished. She was just putting her hairbrush and mirror back, when a knock sounded at her door.

"Coming," Maggie called. She opened the door without thinking to ask who it was. She knew it would be Garrett.

Garrett studied her silently and smiled broadly. "I've seen the other women downstairs, and you'll outshine them all."

Maggie blushed, not knowing what to say. She was quite inexperienced at this type of flattery. Garrett seemed to understand and took her by the hand.

"Let's go to dinner. The train passengers have finished and the dining room will be serving supper to the public." Maggie pulled her door shut and allowed Garrett to lead her down the hall.

The dining room was no shoddy affair. People from town seemed to revel in the finery and quality of Fred Harvey's English taste and decorum. The crystal was spotless, the china without cracks or blemishes, and even the fine linen tablecloths were immaculate.

Maggie ate lobster in a rich cream sauce, as well as baby carrots cooked with grated orange peel, green beans with red pimentos and almond slivers, and a variety of other things she couldn't even remember. After dinner, Garrett suggested a walk.

"Will you be sorry to meet him?" he asked.

"My father?" Maggie inquired, knowing very well the answer.

"Yes. Will you be sorry to meet him again?"

"Sorry? No, not really sorry. I was sorry he had to go away and sorry we both seemed to cause each other such heartache, but I can't honestly say I'll be sorry to meet him again." Maggie went on to tell Garrett about the last time her father had come to Topeka.

"I stole out the back and ran to Lillie's house. Her parents weren't home, but she was. We went to her upstairs bedroom and spied on my father and grandmother as they looked for me. Part of me wanted to run back to him."

"Why didn't you?" Garrett questioned as he assisted Maggie over a missing portion of boardwalk.

"I don't know," she answered softly. Suddenly she didn't want to talk. They strolled in silence for the remainder of their walk.

When they returned to the hotel, Maggie reached into her purse for the key to her room. Without a word, Garrett took it from her and opened the door. "We'll be leaving quite early. I'll ask one of the Harvey girls to wake you in time for breakfast."

The silence fell between them once again, and Maggie felt the intensity of Garrett's stare. Sounds from the restaurant faded away, and even the commotion of hotel guests at the far end of the hall seemed to be in another world.

Garrett stepped forward, and Maggie knew he would kiss her. She wanted him to, yet she remembered her grandmother's warning about being unequally yoked with unbelievers. Grandmother had spoken of men who might court Maggie, but the truth was Maggie was the unbeliever.

Maggie backed into her room abruptly, leaving a surprised Garrett standing with his arms slightly outstretched.

"Good night, Garrett," Maggie whispered and closed the door.

Maggie leaned hard against the door after locking it. She wondered if Garrett was still on the other side. Her heart pounded and her mind was muddled with conflicting emotions. Maggie prepared for bed and hoped sleep would come quickly.

The train ride to Trinidad, Colorado, passed uneventfully. Summer storms had cleared the air, making temperatures quite bearable. The air also became dryer the farther west they traveled. Maggie loved to study the changing landscape. They had passed from rolling prairie hills to parched lands of sagebrush and juniper.

Maggie knew her feelings for Garrett were growing, and Garrett had made it clear how he felt about her. The confusion came because of her own spiritual battle. Maggie didn't want to deal with God or her father, and on the last day of their train journey, she determined to put them both aside and concentrate on her feelings for Garrett.

When dark hues of purple lined the western horizon, Maggie grew curious. "Are those the mountains?" she asked Garrett in little girl excitement.

"Yes, but this distance doesn't do them justice. Wait until we're closer." Garrett shared Maggie's enthusiasm. The mountains meant they were almost home.

Several hours later, Maggie was rewarded with a pristine and glorious sight. The Rocky Mountains in their summer splendor towered majestically before them.

"I've never seen anything like it in all my life. Just look!" Maggie exclaimed as she lowered the train window. She quickly pulled her head back in, as cinders flew back from the smoke stack, stinging her eyes. She tried to fish her handkerchief out of her bag, but it eluded her.

"Here," Garrett offered. "Look at me and I'll get it." Eyes closed, Maggie obediently turned her face to Garrett and allowed him to work.

"There! Good as new," Garrett proclaimed.

When she opened her eyes, Maggie met Garrett's eyes only inches from her own.

"Thank you," she whispered. Desperate to regain her composure, she added, "Does it always look so grand?"

Garrett laughed softly. "Yes, it always does. I find it hard to believe you've never traveled to the mountains before. I'm surprised your grandmother never took you."

"Grandmother wasn't one for traveling. She liked to stay in Topeka, garden whenever possible, and go to church activities."

"I see," Garrett said thoughtfully. "What about you? What did you like to do?"

"Well, let's see. I liked to go to the picnics our church had down by the river. We'd have at least one a month during the summer. I also enjoyed reading and the parties Grandmother and I went to." Maggie poured out the words easily but continued to look out the window, refusing to miss a moment of the newness that passed by.

As the tracks began to climb the steep

grade of Raton Pass, Maggie couldn't help but gasp at the scenery. The mountains rose imposingly on either side, and the evergreens reached for heaven. There was snow on the higher peaks, and wildflowers waved along the tracks.

"We certainly don't have anything like this in Kansas," Maggie said, turning briefly to meet Garrett's eyes.

"That's true," Garrett agreed.

"You must love it a lot," Maggie said thoughtfully.

"Indeed I do. I can only think of one other thing I care more about." Maggie knew Garrett was struggling with his feelings just as she was. They seemed to have an unspoken agreement to leave the subject alone, so Maggie attempted to steer the conversation to safer ground.

"Is my father's ranch this beautiful?"

"Every bit as much and more. It lies in a rich green valley on the other side of the mountains. It's protected on both sides by the Sangre de Cristo range."

"The what?" Maggie questioned, giving Garrett her undivided attention.

"Sangre de Cristo. It means the blood of Christ. Your father said it reminded him of what was important in life. His ranch sits in a deep valley. It's great land for cattle and horses. The Pueblos have a mission not far from the ranch house. Your father set it up for a missionary couple down there. The Pueblos raise fine crops and sheep, and they share portions with your father in exchange for beef," Garrett shared eagerly.

"The Pueblos? Who are they?" Maggie questioned.

"They're Indians. Perfectly harmless," Garrett added at the look of alarm on Maggie's face. "They have a way with irrigation and planting that would make your head spin, and they live in adobe houses like the ranch, only smaller."

"Adobe? I can see I'll have a great deal to learn," Maggie murmured thoughtfully. "We might as well put this time to good use. Tell me about adobe."

"Adobe is an orange clay brick." Garrett was more than happy to teach Maggie about her new life. "The bricks are formed from straw and clay," he continued, "and then allowed to dry in the sun. The adobe is used with a small amount of timber to create a house. Then the workers mud the entire house, filling in the cracks and smoothing over the surface of the walls. The bricks are quite thick and keep the houses well insulated."

"I see, and my father's house is made of

such adobe?"

"That's right. It may not seem as refined as your house in Topeka, but it holds a charm all its own."

"And the interior?" Maggie asked, trying to get a mental picture.

"We don't waste much wood out here, and you won't find a lot of it used in the house. There are some hardwood floors and paneling is used on the walls in a couple of rooms, but usually the stone walls are whitewashed. The interior of your father's house is as nice as any I've seen. I think you'll like it."

"I suppose so," Maggie said softly. She remembered her home in Potwin Place, and how she'd helped her grandmother pick out the colors, wallpaper, and furnishings. "I know it will mean a great deal to my father if I do."

"You don't have to put on a show for him, Maggie," Garrett replied. "Your father is a very simple and very compassionate man. He only asks for honesty."

Maggie stared out the window. The train engine was straining to pull the cars through the tunnel at Raton Pass. They were barely moving.

"I think he expects a bit more than that," Maggie finally said.

"But he won't expect you to put on airs. Just be honest with him, Maggie. He'll want it that way."

The day grew quite warm, and in spite of her excitement, Maggie dozed off and on as they drew nearer her new home.

"Wake up Maggie," Garrett was shaking her shoulder. "We're in Springer."

Maggie jumped up quickly. "I must have fallen asleep."

"I'll say," Garrett drawled in mock sarcasm. "Pert near a three hour nap, little lady."

Maggie laughed. The sound warmed Garrett's heart. It was good to be at peace with Maggie, even though the peace was fragile.

"Will my father be here to greet us?" Maggie questioned, realizing she didn't know.

"He'll be back at the ranch, waiting. He'll have sent the wagons for our gear and some other things we've ordered shipped here," Garrett answered as he pulled his black Stetson on. "Of course, most of the shipment was picked up a couple weeks ago due to our little delay to put you back in order."

Maggie felt a twinge of embarrassment for the detainment. She started to say something but was stopped by Garrett's appearance. She'd never seen him in blue jeans before. His white cotton shirt was open at the neck, and his neatly trimmed beard gave him a mysterious air. Garrett had considered shaving his beard before they left the dugout, but Maggie had protested, telling him it gave him character. Not that Garrett Lucas didn't already have plenty of that, Maggie decided.

When they stepped off the train, Garrett was quickly surrounded by men. They laughed and slapped each other on the back, all talking at once for several minutes. Maggie was certain she'd overheard one of them say congratulations. She wondered if they'd betted on whether Garrett would make it back to New Mexico with her.

Garrett turned quickly to motion Maggie to join them. "Maggie, this is Bill. He's one of your father's right-hand men."

Maggie smiled shyly. "It's nice to meet you," she said softly. The man smiled from ear to ear, revealing several missing teeth. His hair, from what Maggie could see as it peeked out from under a grimy hat, was gray fading to white.

"Pleasure's mine, Miss Maggie!"

He seemed so pleased to meet Maggie that she almost didn't catch the name of the next cowboy as Garrett had her meet the entire crew.

"This is Mack, this tall, scraggly looking

126

guy is Cactus Jack, and this old good-for-nothing is Pike." Garrett whirled Maggie around the circle. They all seemed happy to meet her and so genuine in their greetings and best wishes that Maggie felt warmly welcomed.

"Joe and Willy are waiting for us at Five Mile Junction," Bill announced to Garrett.

"Well, it's nearly noon, and I'd imagine if we're going to make Five Mile Junction by night, we'd better get a move on," Garrett announced. It was clear to Maggie from the response of the cowboys that Garrett was in charge.

Maggie tried to take everything in: the countryside, the town, the people. Springer was the county seat, but it was much smaller than Topeka.

She stood to one side watching a hired carriage pull away with a distinguished looking man and woman. The woman was fussing with her ill-fitting traveling clothes, and the bored man was studying the head of his cane. It appeared life was the same all over. Maggie couldn't help but smile to herself.

"Do you need to stop for anything before we get on the road?" Garrett was asking.

"No, I don't think so," Maggie replied, trying to think of anything she might need.

"There's a small trading post north of the

ranch. We usually get supplies and anything else we need from there. If you think of something once you get home, let somebody know and we can add it to the list. Someone is always heading over to the post office every few weeks," Garrett explained.

"We'll be that far removed from civilization?" Maggie questioned, not realizing her look of astonishment.

"I never thought of it that way," Garrett answered thoughtfully. "I guess I never needed anything more, so it didn't seem so uncivilized."

"I didn't mean to insult the place," Maggie said apologetically. "I just presumed we'd live near town. I never thought much about my father's place."

Garrett helped Maggie into the wagon and easily jumped in to take a seat beside her.

"Well, you'll have a few days' ride to consider it." With that, Garrett gave the reins a flick and the horses took their place behind Mack's wagon.

The wagon wasn't nearly as comfortable as the train had been, and while the scenery was of intense interest, Maggie's backside was sorely abused from the rocky pathway they called a road.

Two hours later, they stopped to eat. The rest was quite brief, however, and Maggie soon found herself back on the dusty trail headed into the mountains of the Sangre de Cristo.

Maggie was disappointed with the countryside. From the train, the land had seemed greener and less sandy. Up close, it looked like the edge of a desert. Maggie hoped her father's ranch would be different.

As the sun passed behind the mountain peaks and the sky took on a purple hue, Maggie grew quite chilly. As if reading her mind, Garrett halted the wagon long enough to take a blanket out from under the wagon seat.

"Here, this ought to help. We're almost to Five Mile Junction." Garrett helped Maggie pull the blanket around her shoulders.

Little more than a gathering of shacks and corrals, Five Mile Junction looked wonderful to Maggie. After a delicious supper of steak, potatoes, biscuits, and pie, Maggie was shown to a small room. She'd changed into her nightgown and was brushing out her waist-long hair when a knock sounded at the door.

"Yes?"

"It's me, Maggie," Garrett announced. "May I come in?"

"Of course, just one minute," she said as

she pulled on her robe. "Alright, come ahead."

Garrett sucked his breath in hard as he caught sight of Maggie illuminated by candle. She was so delicate, yet her strength astounded him. And if all went well, one day she'd be his.

"You're so beautiful," he said in a husky whisper.

Maggie lowered her gaze, refusing to meet his eyes. She could feel a blush coloring her cheeks.

Garrett closed the space between them in two strides. He stood directly in front of Maggie without touching her. Maggie lifted her eyes to meet his. Words seemed inadequate, yet both felt captive to a spell. A spell that needed to be broken.

Garrett took a step back. "This trip is getting rougher all the time." Maggie nodded. "Tomorrow, we've got a lot of ground to cover in a short time. Are you up to it?" Again Maggie nodded, finding it hard to speak.

"Good. I'll have the cook wake you at five."

Garrett took another step back. He wanted so much to hold Maggie in his arms. No one would have to know, no one but them — and God. The thought caused Garrett to remember their future depended on more than physical attraction. He walked to the door and, with one last glance, pulled it shut behind him and breathed a sigh of relief.

CHAPTER 10

Maggie couldn't remember a rougher ride or a more desolate land. Aside from sagebrush and scrawny trees, Maggie could see nothing to break the monotonous, dusty brown earth. How could her father love this country?

Garrett concentrated on steering the team through the narrow, rocky pass. He was growing painfully aware of Maggie's presence as she bounced back and forth in the wagon seat. He needed a way to distance himself from her long enough for Jason to have a chance to get to know his daughter.

"Is this all there is to it?" Maggie questioned disappointedly as she gazed from side to side.

"What do you mean?" Garrett asked.

"All of this," Maggie said, motioning to the landscape. "I thought you said it was beautiful."

"Your home is beautiful. You'll see. This is

just the way we get there," Garrett answered stiffly. The lead teams were slowing to a stop, and Garrett reined back on his team. "Whoa, whoa boys," he called softly.

"Why are we stopping?" Maggie inquired, forgetting the scenery.

"We'll water the horses here. They've had a long, hard haul," Garrett answered rather curtly.

"Garrett?" Maggie said his name, and Garrett swallowed hard. She was charming without being aware of it. Her cheeks were red from the wind, and her hair had come loose and hung in curled wisps around her face.

"Have I done something wrong?" Maggie questioned earnestly. "Is it because I don't like the land?"

Lifting Maggie from the wagon, Garrett looked deep into her sapphire eyes framed by long, sooty lashes. Why did he notice every detail about her? How could she be more beautiful out here than she'd been back in Kansas?

"Wrong? The land?" he whispered hoarsely. "I don't know what you're talking about," he lied and instantly regretted it. His hands lingered around her waist for a moment. Then he turned as if to leave.

"You've hardly said two words to me all

day. If I've done something wrong, I have a right to know it." Maggie's words were a little harsher than she'd intended.

Garrett fought to control his emotions. How could he wait a year or more for Maggie to grow up and marry him? What if some other young man swept her heart away before he had a chance to insure that it belonged to him?

"I have to water the horses," Garrett said and walked away.

"Well!" Maggie huffed and turned to go for a walk. She climbed up the rocky ledge and became so winded that she had to sit down and catch her breath. Garrett had warned her about the altitude and how it would take time to get used to.

As she regained normal breathing, Maggie climbed the rock and marveled at the dainty wildflowers that sprinkled the ground around her. From the wagon, she'd been sure this land was devoid of any beauty.

She reached down and picked a frilly yellow flower that matched the gown she was wearing. After fingering the lacy edges of the flower, she tucked it in the lace lining the yoke of her bodice. She loved the feel of the mountain breeze through her hair and pulled loose the ribbon that tied back the bulk of her auburn hair. What a feeling!

Perhaps this arid land had something to offer.

As she reached a small rocky ledge, Maggie was rewarded with a splendid view of the Sangre de Cristo. The snowcapped summit of the highest peak glistened and beckoned to her. She almost felt like she was coming home.

"Maggie!" Garrett's voice intruded on her thoughts.

What was bothering him? Maggie worked her way down the rocky path again. "I've done nothing to cause him grief," she muttered to herself as she checked her steps, remembering to walk from side to side as Garrett had taught her.

"Where have you been?" Garrett snapped. His eyes narrowed and grew darker. "I've been looking all over for you!"

"I just took a walk, that's all," Maggie answered calmly. She wasn't going to let Garrett Lucas cause her to lose her temper.

"You make sure somebody knows where you're going before you go heading off somewhere." Maggie bit her lower lip until she tasted blood. Garrett continued to scold her as if she were a child. "This isn't like Topeka. This country is wild and unpredictable."

"It's not alone," Maggie muttered.

"Just what's that supposed to mean?" Garrett questioned. He was already mad at himself for allowing his frustration to distance Maggie.

"It means you've never answered my question, and I don't understand why you're treating me so cruelly." Maggie stood against the sun, her jaw set. "Now are you going to give me an answer?"

Garrett reached out and took Maggie in his arms. He bent his lips to hers and had barely touched them when he pulled back and walked away. A few feet down the path, he turned on his heel, returned to Maggie, and kissed her soundly. Maggie could feel the dampness of his sweat-soaked shirt and the powerful muscles of his protective arms. Suddenly, Garrett pulled himself away and strode back to the team.

Maggie stared at his retreating back. *I guess that's the only answer I'll get,* she thought. *But what an answer.* After a few minutes, she joined Garrett at the wagon and allowed him to help her up.

"Mack's going to drive you," Garrett said and walked away.

Maggie was truly confused. If her company was so unpleasant, why had Garrett kissed her? And if it wasn't because of a distaste for her company, why had he sent

Mack to drive the team?

Mack turned out to be a pleasant traveling companion. He was young and energetic like Garrett, but he wasn't Garrett. Mack told Maggie stories about cattle drives and growing up in Texas.

Maggie felt badly that she only half-listened. She was still consumed by questions about Garrett's attitude. She asked Mack why Garrett had requested him to trade wagons, but Mack only shrugged his shoulders and told her he was just following orders.

The day passed quickly, and when evening came, Maggie asked Mack, "Where will we stay the night?"

"Out here under the stars, Miss Maggie," he answered, surprised that she didn't already know.

"Oh, I see," she said, looking around her.

Moments later they stopped for the night. The men quickly unharnessed the horses, rubbing them down and giving them feed and water. Bill made a supper fire while Mack and Cactus Jack unloaded food and water.

Maggie felt totally useless. She didn't know the first thing about camping, and she couldn't find out where Garrett had gone. After about an hour, Bill announced supper was as fit as it was going to get, and the party gathered around the fire to eat.

"Where is Garrett?" Maggie questioned, unable to contain her curiosity.

"He's on the ridge, Miss Maggie," Bill offered the words along with a tin plate of beans and warm spiced apples. "He'll keep the first watch of the night."

"Oh," Maggie whispered. She wondered what he was keeping watch over, but she was too fearful of the answer to ask. Was it animals or people? Perhaps it was the banditos Mack had told her of. Maggie shivered.

"You'd better sit here by the fire, Miss Maggie," Bill directed, motioning her to a blanket. "I'll bring you some biscuits and dried beef to go with that. How 'bout some coffee to wash it all down with?" The older man worried over her like a father.

"No, thank you. Water would be fine."

"Whatever you like, little lady," Bill said and was on the move to bring Maggie her water.

Supper passed quickly, and much to Maggie's surprise, the men went about cleaning up the dishes and leftovers without looking once in Maggie's direction for help. When she offered to dry the plates, Bill waved her off.

138

It was growing cold when Maggie realized she'd left her shawl in the wagon. She remembered Garrett's earlier rebuke about not announcing her whereabouts and decided she'd better tell Bill where she was headed.

"Bill, I'm going to the wagon to get my shawl."

"Better take some light. There's hardly enough moon to see by tonight," Bill replied, looking up at the starry sky. Maggie nodded.

"Just grab ya some fire." Bill motioned to the campfire and went about his business.

In her seventeen years, Maggie had never had to pull a stick from a fire, and she wasn't sure how to go about it. She stood by the fire, wanting to ask one of the hands for help, but they were busy. She finally gave up and went to the wagon in the dark.

Maggie had just reached the wagon when she heard the lonely howl of a coyote. Maggie thought of her home in Topeka and wondered if her grandmother was lonely. She had Two Moons, but it wouldn't be the same. Grandmother loved conversation, and Two Moons rarely spoke.

There was also Lillie. Maggie missed her badly. It would be fun to share her adventures with Lillie when she got a chance to write.

Maggie carefully placed her foot on a wheel spoke and pulled herself to the top of the wagon. She climbed in back with little effort and was feeling rather proud of herself when she heard a low growling sound somewhere behind her.

She turned to see two greenish yellow eyes staring back at her. Maggie felt a scream in her throat, but it wouldn't release. Motionless, she watched and waited as the growling intensified. Her breath came in quick gasps, and her heart pounded.

"Garrett!" She managed to scream the name, causing the growling to stop for a moment. "Garrett!"

Maggie saw the eyes lunge at the wagon. She heard the impact of the animal as it hit the wooden side and the commotion of the men at the campfire.

Maggie had never been given to fainting, but she had never faced such fear. As she passed into unconsciousness, she heard a single gunshot ring out, then nothing.

"Maggie? Maggie, are you alright?" Garrett called as he held her against his chest. Maggie felt herself floating. Finally, she opened her eyes. Someone had brought a lantern, and she heard Garrett assure the other men she was okay.

"It's alright, Bill. She's not hurt," Garrett announced. "I think that coyote might be rabid or elsewise she got into some loco weed. Better check it out." Bill took the hint and motioned the rest of the ranch hands to follow him.

"Come on, boys. We've got a coyote to skin." Bill continued to talk to his companions as they walked back to camp, but Maggie was only aware of Garrett and the protection she felt.

"I'm beginning to wonder if I'm going to get you to your father alive," Garrett said as he held Maggie.

"I'm sorry. I told Bill where I was going. Honest, I did," Maggie said, struggling to meet Garrett's eyes.

"I know, Bill told me. But he also told you to take a light."

"I didn't know how to get the stick out of the fire," Maggie admitted in a defeated voice. "I didn't want to be a bother."

Garrett threw back his head and laughed. "That coyote didn't mind the bother," he finally said. "The fire would've kept him at his distance."

"I didn't know," Maggie said, feeling utterly dejected. How could she know what was expected of her in this new world?

"Oh, *mi querida,* you are a prize," Garrett whispered as he ran a finger along her jaw. "I wish I could go straight to Pastor David and have him marry us."

Maggie sat up rather abruptly. "But I thought you and Father planned for me, I mean us, to marry right away."

Garrett grinned. "I'd like that more than I can say, but that isn't the plan."

"What then?" Maggie questioned.

"You need to get to know your father, and —" He paused for a moment. "You need to do some growing up."

"Growing up? Well, I never. I wouldn't be the first woman to get married at seventeen. Besides, on July 24th I'll be eighteen!" Maggie exclaimed, squaring her shoulders.

"Maggie, you need to learn about life, and you need to be a daughter before you become a wife." Garrett noticed the disappointment in Maggie's expression. "It's funny how just a few weeks ago you were all spit and fire, hating me with your eyes if not your words. Now you can't understand why you can't be my wife. Maggie, have you ever thought of the responsibilities of a wife?"

Maggie blushed deeply. Garrett smiled as if reading her mind.

"I know how to cook, clean, sew, and most

everything else a good wife would need to know," Maggie said, avoiding Garrett's eyes. "I hardly see what being a daughter has to do with being a good wife."

"It has a great deal to do with it, Maggie. Why wouldn't you have much to do with gentlemen callers?"

"How dare you delve into my personal life!" Maggie was indignant.

"Don't you think a husband should know such things?" Garrett inquired softly.

"But you aren't my husband, and it doesn't sound like you want to be," Maggie pouted. A spark of hope flared as she wondered if she could entice Garrett to marry her immediately. If she arrived on the ranch as Mrs. Garrett Lucas, perhaps she wouldn't have to deal so intensely with her father.

Garrett looked seriously at Maggie as he turned her to face him. "Magdelena Intissar, you'd better knock off the little girl theatrics and listen up. You will never be the woman you were meant to be as long as you don't reconcile your relationship with your Heavenly Father. You've never accepted Jesus as your Savior, and you'll never be happy without Him. But, just like with your father, that relationship is a personal one. One that I can't interfere with or get for

143

you. You'll have to take it one step at a time, on your own."

Maggie lowered her eyes. "I just don't know if I can, Garrett." Garrett pulled her tightly against him.

"I know you can," he breathed against her soft hair.

"Will you help me?"

Garrett was quiet for a moment. When he spoke, Maggie felt her heart nearly break. "No, I can't. I won't be there."

Maggie tore herself from his grasp. "You won't be there? Then where will you be?" she demanded.

"I'm going away. That way you'll have to deal with your father and with God. I'll be nearby, but I won't be influencing your decisions and actions. You won't be so confused then."

"Just how do you know what I'll be and won't be? Garrett Lucas, I think you're a cruel man. How could you take me away from my home, thrust me into the presence of someone I don't know, and expect me to handle the situation alone?"

"But Maggie, you won't be alone. God will go with you."

"God doesn't appear to have come with me this far," Maggie said, immediately regretting the words.

144

"Maggie, you don't believe that. I know your words were spoken out of fear, but I'm telling you that you have nothing to fear. Your father adores you. He's missed you every day of your separation. You won't find it hard to span the years. I promise. And as for Jesus — well, He's been standing with open arms all your life."

"Words. Just words," Maggie said, pulling herself to her feet. "I'm in exactly the same position I was years ago: on my own, to stand alone. You probably won't come back." Her voice gave way to a sob.

Garrett was beside her in a flash. "I'll be back. Don't ever doubt it. I'm going to marry you one day, Maggie Intissar, and that is something you can most definitely count on."

Surprising herself and Garrett, Maggie jumped over the side of the wagon and headed toward the campfire light.

"I mean it, Maggie. Don't ever doubt me," Garrett called after her. Maggie kept going.

Taking a blanket Bill offered, she rested on the makeshift bed Bill had prepared from pine needles and blankets. She refused to let the men see her cry, but long after the sounds of heavy breathing and snoring filled the air, another sound joined the night. It was the sound of Maggie's intense, muffled

sobs — cries that did not escape Garrett
Lucas.

CHAPTER 11

The next day, Maggie was riding with Bill when they paused at the opening of the valley her father ranched. Maggie stared in awe.

Piñon Canyon, as the ranch was called, stretched for miles. The burnt orange adobe ranch house contrasted sharply with the sturdy green piñon pines, which grew in abundance in the valley. Other, smaller buildings dotted the landscape, and several huge corrals stood in direct angles from the house. Beyond the inner circle of the ranch threaded a wide, silvery stream.

"I can hardly believe it," Maggie said in wonder. "I never would've guessed something so heavenly could be hidden in the middle of the desolation we've been riding through. It's beautiful!"

"That it is, Miss Maggie. I've called it home for nearly twelve years now, and it's always a welcome sight," Bill said enthusiastically.

"Twelve years? But my father has only been in the territory for eight years."

"That's so, but I worked this ranch for the former owner. Course it weren't nothing like what your pa has made of it. It was just a little stomping ground then. I was one of only three hands. Your father keeps over fifty." Bill urged the horses forward with a flick of the reins.

"Fifty? Why does my father need so many people?" Maggie questioned, suddenly wanting to know everything.

"There's enough work for fifty people, so he hired fifty," Bill said in his joking manner. "See, there's a lot more to a ranch than meets the eye. Somebody's got to keep up with the herd's feeding, watering, herding, branding, medicating, and such. Then there's those who keep up the land and the property. Those fences didn't just put themselves up, and they don't stay up without help. Not to mention the house help."

"I get the picture, Bill," Maggie laughed. Then, more seriously, she asked, "What's my father like?"

"I think pretty highly of your pa. He's an honest man, pays a fair wage, and sees to it that no one goes without. He even keeps a mission on the property. It's over that ridge, 'bout twelve miles. He supports the minister and his wife who keep it up for the Pueblos."

"Oh yes, the Indians," Maggie tried to sound intelligent.

"That's right. Your pa looks after everybody."

"But why? Why does he care so much?" Maggie wondered aloud.

"I 'spect it has to do with what your pa is always saying. God was good to him, so he'll just pass it on and be good to others." Bill fell silent, and Maggie didn't ask anything else.

The day passed quickly, and after several stops to rest and water the horses, the travelers were in the valley, making their way down the well-worn path which led to Piñon Canyon.

As they approached the first corral, several brown-skinned cowboys came riding up on horseback. They rode alongside Garrett talking in Spanish and laughing. Some fell back to greet the others and cast glances at Maggie. While she couldn't understand what they said, their smiles and excitement led her to believe she'd passed inspection.

Maggie suddenly grew self-conscious about her appearance. She was wearing the same yellow dress she'd had on for days. She was freckled and sunburned, and her hair hung in a lifeless braid down her back. What would her father think?

Once again, Maggie began to fear her reunion with her father. What if Jason Intissar had love and kindness for everyone except his daughter? What if she still stirred painful memories of her mother? Maggie had been told by her grandmother that she resembled her mother more than ever. What if her father couldn't deal with the haunting image?

In less than a heartbeat, the group halted at the huge stone walkway leading to the double doors of the ranch house. Maggie wanted to run. Her eyes darted around, and she gripped the side of the wagon. The muscles in her chest tightened, making normal breathing impossible.

Just then, Maggie caught Garrett's sympathetic look. He winked at her as Bill helped her from the wagon. The ranch house doors opened, and Jason Intissar burst through.

"Magdelena! You're really here! Oh, my Maggie, my daughter!" Maggie's father embraced her tightly. She could feel his bony thinness.

Jason stepped back to eye his daughter. Maggie said nothing. The feelings she'd buried so long ago, feelings of an eight-year-old girl watching her father walk away, threatened to overwhelm her. She wanted to say something, but her mouth refused to form the words.

"Oh, Maggie. It's really me." Jason laughed, hoping the assurance would help Maggie put aside her worried expression. "I've missed you so much! I can't believe you're finally here." Jason took her hand and twirled her in a circle before him. Maggie felt her body mechanically respond, but her heart was too overwhelmed to allow rational thought.

"You're more beautiful than your painting. Your mama would be proud. You look just like her. My, but how I miss her, *mi querida*."

"That phrase — what does it mean?" Maggie questioned.

Jason smiled and took hold of her hand, "Desired one, my daughter. Just as you are to me."

Maggie raised an eyebrow, remembering Garrett's use of the phrase but said nothing, noting the sadness in Jason's eyes.

Garrett Lucas broke the spell. "Well, Jason, here she is. I knew it would be worth the effort, didn't you?" Garrett's words were both sincere and mocking. Maggie flashed fiery eyes at him, but Garrett's lazy grin and laughing eyes were too much. She looked away.

"It was worth the effort and the wait. How do I thank you, my dear friend?" Jason exclaimed, turning to grab Garrett's hand with his free one.

"You've already rewarded me by promising me your daughter in marriage," Garrett said casually. He stared intently at Maggie until she could feel herself blush from head to toe.

"Garrett!" Jason cried. Garrett waved his concern away.

"She knows all about it. She's even happy about it. She just doesn't like the waiting," Garrett said, pushing back the brim of his hat. Maggie fumed at the nonchalant way in which Garrett treated their betrothal.

"Is this true, Maggie?" Jason questioned. Maggie was touched by the deep concern in her father's voice. She allowed her eyes to meet his. He was grayer than she'd remembered, and his shoulders seemed more stooped. He wasn't an old man, but the sickness had taken its toll. And, try as she might, Maggie couldn't find a reason to hate her father any longer.

"Maggie, is it true you're willing to marry Garrett?" her father asked pleadingly.

Maggie squared her shoulders and looked first to Garrett. He was actually enjoying this moment. He raised a mocking eyebrow as if to mimic her father's question. Maggie let go of her father's hand. She thought of denying it all, but when she saw the anguish in her father's eyes, she couldn't.

"Yes," she whispered and turned her eyes to the smooth stone beneath her feet.

"Praise God!" her father exclaimed. "I had only hoped to dare that this marriage might take place. Oh, what happy news the two of you have brought me."

Maggie felt defeated and tired. She wanted to get even with Garrett, but she didn't have the energy to fight back.

The warmth of the noon sun was bearing down on them, and Jason motioned them to the house. "Come on. We need to get you out of this heat. I'll bet you'd like a bath," Jason said, taking hold of Maggie's arm and leading her into the house.

Garrett had been right, as usual. She loved the interior of the ranch as much as she'd loved the outside. Her father had made it warm and cheery with vast amounts of Indian pottery and fresh flowers. Indian blankets woven from coarse wool in intricate and colorful patterns were hanging from the walls.

Jason began showing Maggie first one thing, then another. The dining room was richly warm with wooden floors and dark cherry furniture. Heavy brocade draperies at the large windows blocked out the hot afternoon sun.

Maggie barely heard her father's words as he explained the meaning behind different pieces of furniture. It was all she could do to comprehend that she was in her father's house and Garrett was going to leave.

Finally, Maggie spoke. "Please, could I see it all later? I'm so tired."

"Forgive me, of course. I'm just so anxious for you to feel at home here," Jason said as he paused to embrace Maggie once again. "I love you, my little Maggie. Welcome home."

Maggie felt strange going to bed in the middle of the day, but her father had explained that everyone took a siesta during the heat of the day. She found a bath drawn for her, and once she'd bathed and donned a soft cotton nightgown, she was shown to her bed by Carmalita, the young woman who was to be her maid.

Carmalita was young, perhaps twenty or so, Maggie judged. She was plump and very pretty. Maggie immediately liked her.

"We've looked forward to your arrival,

Miss Magdelena." Carmalita spoke perfect English, although her accent betrayed her Mexican heritage.

"Please, just call me Maggie and don't be so formal. I find myself in need of new friends and hope to start with you," Maggie said sincerely.

"I would be most honored to call you friend, Miss — Maggie." Carmalita replied softly. There weren't many women on the ranch, and Maggie was a welcomed change.

"Good. I will rely on you to teach me everything, but first I want to sleep," Maggie yawned and laid back against the softness of down pillows.

"I will wake you for afternoon refreshments," Carmalita replied gently as she closed the door behind her.

Maggie surveyed the room. It looked out of place with the rest of the house. The room was clearly designed with a woman's tastes in mind. The walls were papered in a lavender rose print. Lavender shutters were closed tightly over a window. French doors with lavender ruffled curtains were set in an archway. Maggie wondered where the doors led, but weariness kept her from exploring.

Suddenly, she began to think of Garrett. Did he really mean to leave? And what of her father's contentment as he'd bidden her pleasant dreams? He seemed so genuinely happy to have her home.

Home. Strange that one word should stir so many different feelings. Home had always meant Topeka, yet Maggie felt torn. Coming to this mountainous paradise had been like coming home. How did one explain such feelings?

Maggie shook off the worries of the past few weeks and closed her eyes. She fervently wished she could put Garrett's smiling face from her mind, but it refused to leave. Exhausted, she gave up and slept, oblivious to the conversation taking place in her father's study.

"Garrett, it's so good to have you back," a wearied Jason was exclaiming as he weakly lowered himself to a chair.

"Good to be back, although I wondered at times if we'd make it."

"She was pretty ornery, was she?" Jason laughingly asked.

"She was everything you warned me of, and more. Did you know I had to pull her off a two-story trellis?" Garrett smiled as he remembered the scene and quickly joined Jason's hearty laugh.

"I'm not kidding. Sophia had warned me that Maggie would make a run for it. I figured somebody looking as prim and proper as your daughter would sneak down the back stairs or hide in another room until she could slip out the front, but not Maggie. She hiked up her skirts, all those petticoats and such, and stepped as pretty as you please out her bedroom window and onto the trellis."

Jason alternated between laughing and coughing.

"Maybe I should stop," Garrett said, concerned about Jason's condition. The older man's health had rapidly deteriorated during Garrett's absence.

"No, please. I want to know. I need to hear it all," Jason said, the smile never leaving his face. " 'A merry heart doeth good like a medicine,' the Scripture says. Now continue so my heart can have a good dosing."

Garrett chuckled in spite of his concern. "Well, there she was, picking her way through the roses and lattice work, all the while yelling about the injustice of life. I wouldn't have seen her up there, if I hadn't heard her first. Quite a set of lungs on your daughter, Sir."

Jason fairly howled at this. "Got it from her mother," he gasped.

"I'm sure." Garrett winked and continued. "Anyway, when she got close enough, I reached up and grabbed her."

"She didn't see you?" Jason coughed the words. He hadn't enjoyed himself this much for years.

"No, Sir," Garrett managed while holding his side and laughing. "She doesn't see as much when her mouth is open."

"At any rate," Jason said, trying to compose himself. "You're here. Through all the trials and Maggie's stubbornness, you've managed to bring my daughter back to me. Thank you so much."

"You know how I feel about it, Jason. I love your daughter more than ever." Garrett's declaration nearly moved Jason to tears.

"Strange how quickly a body can pass from hilarity into sober reflection," Jason murmured thoughtfully. "I think I'll follow my advice to Maggie and take a nap. This has taken a lot out of me." Jason struggled to get to his feet, and Garrett offered him a steady hand.

"Sounds like an excellent idea," Garrett agreed. "First though, I'll see to you."

Garrett helped Jason into bed and walked toward the bedroom door. That's when it caught his eye. The life-sized portrait of Maggie hung in regal splendor across from Jason's bed. Garrett paused to study the teasing smile and passionate blue eyes. He wanted to grow old with that smile. Turning to leave, Garrett couldn't resist smiling back.

CHAPTER 12

Maggie woke several hours later to Carmalita's gentle nudge. She stretched leisurely thinking she hadn't slept so well in weeks.

"You will find Señor, your father, has thoughtfully purchased all the things you will need," Carmalita remarked, opening the doors of a huge mahogany wardrobe.

Maggie gasped. "There are so many clothes!" she said. There were gowns for every occasion possible, as well as some native-style skirts and peasant blouses. Maggie found these particularly interesting.

"Señor thought you might like them," Carmalita offered. "It gets quite warm here, and they are most comfortable."

"I can't imagine it gets much hotter than Kansas. There were days when you scarcely could move from the heat," Maggie said. Could it have only been weeks since she'd been safe in her own room in Topeka?

Maggie found riding outfits with long split

skirts, petticoats, and light-weight camisoles. Just when Maggie thought she'd seen everything, Carmalita would open a drawer or pull Maggie along to another chest. Maggie was amazed. She found boots, slippers, gloves, shawls, and things she'd never thought about owning.

"Carmalita, how in the world did my father arrange for these things? How did he know they would fit?"

"Señor had your former dressmaker send your measurements. Then he ordered materials, and I made them into clothing. Of course, I had help and some things we ordered from the catalog."

"I see," Maggie said.

"Come, you must select something. Your father will expect you to join him and Señor Garrett for tea."

"Oh, he will? Perhaps I should decline and show them both they can't anticipate my actions." Carmalita looked puzzled, and Maggie put aside the notion of causing a disturbance at Carmalita's expense.

"I'll wear this," Maggie said, taking a white cotton peasant blouse and colorful skirt. Carmalita smiled broadly at this sign of acceptance.

"Come. I'll show you how to wear them." Several minutes later, Maggie surveyed her image in the dressing table mirror. "I look so different, almost wild." she observed. Her hair hung down to her waist in auburn waves.

"How would you like to wear your hair?" Carmalita questioned. "I am quite good at dressing hair."

"I think I prefer to leave it down for now. I might as well go completely casual," Maggie murmured.

Carmalita left and returned with Mexican sandals. "These will make your outfit complete," she said, handing the sandals to Maggie.

"They are beautiful. I've never seen anything like them." Maggie sat down while Carmalita showed her how to put them on.

"Oh, they're so comfortable. I love them, Carmalita."

Carmalita smiled more broadly than ever, but mindful of the time, she motioned Maggie to follow. "Come. Your father is waiting."

"And Señor Garrett?" Maggie questioned sarcastically.

"Si. Your *novio* is waiting," Carmalita answered as she guided Maggie down a long hallway.

"My what?" Maggie asked Carmalita in a hushed whisper.

"Your fiancé. Your sweetheart. You are to marry Señor Garrett, is it not so?" Carmalita questioned.

Maggie rolled her eyes and pushed back a long strand of hair. "I suppose everyone knows about this arrangement." It was more a statement than a question, and Carmalita said nothing as she led Maggie down the long corridor.

"Finally!" Jason Intissar exclaimed loudly as Maggie stepped into the room. Garrett turned from the fireplace and swallowed hard. The look on his face told Maggie that her appearance had taken its planned toll. *Good,* Maggie thought. *I hope he realizes what he's throwing away. I am not to be put aside like a child's toy.*

"Child, you're positively radiant. The climate agrees with you. Did Carmalita show you everything?" Maggie's father questioned eagerly. He hugged Maggie warmly.

Maggie wanted to respond to her father's embrace, but caution flooded her heart and she stood perfectly still. If the reaction pained Jason, he said nothing.

"Garrett and I were discussing your trip. I'm so glad you gave up your plans to run away. You could have been killed, Maggie." Jason's words were full of concern. He didn't sound condemning as Maggie had expected.

"I did what I felt I had to do," Maggie said, taking a seat in the woven cane chair that Jason offered her. An uncomfortable stillness blanketed the room.

Jason broke the silence. "Well, you're here now, and I pray you'll be happy. I've done everything I could think of to welcome you and make you comfortable. I know Carmalita showed you the clothes, but there is more than that. I had special furniture made for your room, I've had several geldings made available for your choice of mount, and I've tried to prepare an abundance of reading materials in the library."

"That was quite thoughtful of you, Father. However, it wasn't necessary. While I've never had to live without the things I needed, I am not like most well-to-do women. I can live quite simply if I need to." Maggie lifted her chin in a defiant move her grandmother would have recognized as a warning.

"Maggie, we need to talk. We three," Jason said, motioning toward Garrett. Maggie stared icily in Garrett's direction. "Pray continue, Father," she said with slight sarcasm.

"Stop it, Maggie. Your father deserves better than one of your temper tantrums," an angry Garrett stated. "He's only trying to make it easy on you. Now stop acting like a spoiled child."

"You seem rather intent on making an issue of my age. As I've told you before, I will be eighteen in less than three weeks. Most of my friends are married, and some even have children. I am not a child, nor do I act childish. I am, however, running out of patience with this game.

"I am here, Father. Not by my wishes, but by Garrett Lucas's and yours. I am not happy I had to leave Grandmother. She's an old woman, and her health is failing. Now she will live out her days alone, and I resent that." Maggie paused briefly to note the expression of surprise on her father's face.

Maggie didn't want to hurt her father, but overpowering fear was gripping her heart. She didn't want to remember thoughts and feelings that were threatening to surface. Anger seemed the only way to hold them at bay.

"Does my ability to speak for myself surprise you? Did you think I'd come running back for the happy reunion? I don't hate you as I once did." Maggie heard her father gasp and regretted her words. But it was too late.

"Yes, that's right. I did hate you," Maggie said the words to her father, but it was Garrett she was thinking of. Garrett and his plans to desert her just as her father had, just as God had.

"You left me. I had just lost my mother and the baby brother I had yearned for, then you turned and walked away. I was ridiculed as an orphan. The few friends I had pitied my loss and my life. My only hope was in Grandmother. She stood by me and held me when I was afraid. She kept me on the narrow path when I felt sure I would stray." Tears threatened to spill from Maggie's eyes. She could see her father, too, had tears. Garrett, however, remained strangely still.

Maggie softened her voice. "I don't hate you anymore. Garrett told me why you left, and while I suppose Grandmother tried to explain it to me many times, Garrett finally accomplished getting through to me. I won't pretend I'm not fearful of this entire arrangement, and while it's true I have come to accept the idea of marriage to your choice of a husband," she said, waving her hand toward Garrett, "I don't believe the man in question has the same desire."

Garrett's lips curled into a smile. Jason

looked first to Garrett, then back to Maggie before both he and Garrett burst into laughter. "Oh, Maggie, you have no idea." Jason's words stung.

"Then why don't you fill me in? Or don't I have a right to know what is to become of me?" Maggie's words were devoid of emotion. Everything inside her went numb.

Jason started to speak, but Garrett raised his hand. "I told you before, Maggie. I fully intend to marry you, but it will be in my own good time and after you've made peace with your father and God."

Jason said nothing, and Maggie noticed he strained to breathe. She didn't want to fight the sick, frail man her father had become.

Maggie turned to face Garrett. "I have spent a lifetime distancing myself from painful relationships. If what you said to me last night was true, then I am about to begin that task once again."

"But, Maggie," Jason interjected. "Garrett loves you. If you can't see that, you're blind. He's trying to tell you that we need to break down the wall between us. It hurts me so much to see you like this, Maggie."

"I can't pretend to be what I'm not. Nor can I conjure feelings that aren't there," Maggie spoke slowly. "I can't forget what happened, and I don't think you can either."

"What are you talking about?" Jason questioned earnestly.

Maggie wasn't sure. More than a feeling, a vague memory filled her mind. It had to be quite terrible, Maggie decided, or her mind would let her remember.

"Never mind," Maggie replied firmly. Something kept her from continuing. "As for you, Garrett Lucas, either you want to marry me or you don't. You have no right to put me off."

Garrett toyed with an Indian pitcher. He smiled slightly as he traced the pattern etched on the pitcher's side. "You mean like you're putting off your father and God?"

Maggie jumped to her feet. "Stop it! I won't tolerate any more of this!" She walked quickly from the room, nearly running by the time she approached the long hallway. She suddenly realized she had no idea where she was going. Tears blinded her, causing her to stumble. Strong hands steadied her, and in a heartbeat, Maggie felt herself held firmly in Garrett Lucas's arms.

"Leave me alone!" she exclaimed in a half sob. She jerked wildly, trying to escape.

"When are you going to give this up? Trust me, I know what I'm doing," Garrett whispered in Maggie's ear.

Maggie went limp against Garrett's chest. "You can't leave me here. I don't know him. I don't know how to live here," Maggie sobbed.

"You'll learn and do so much faster and more thoroughly without me here. Remember, until a few weeks ago, you didn't know me either. Now you're ready to commit your life to me."

"I don't believe you! I don't believe you will come back. You'll be just like him. You'll walk away and keep going." Maggie's words tore at Garrett's heart.

"Hush," he said softly, as he stroked Maggie's hair. "I'm sorry, *mi querida.* I never thought about it that way." Gently he lifted her tearstained face to meet his searching gaze. "I promise, Maggie. I promise you we'll be man and wife one day. I won't leave without returning to claim what is mine. But," he paused, losing himself in the liquid blue of her eyes. "I don't believe you can ever be mine until you resolve your feelings toward your father. I know too we can't be anything to each other until you come to salvation in Jesus."

Maggie pushed away from Garrett's embrace. She squared her shoulders and wiped her eyes. There was a new composure about her, and Garrett showed his surprise.

"When will you leave?" Maggie calmly questioned.

Garrett said nothing for a moment, as if considering her question. Finally, he spoke the word Maggie dreaded. "Tomorrow."

Maggie smoothed the front of her skirt and lifted a stony face. "As you wish. Garrett Lucas, I release you from any commitment you think we might have between us. I'm on my own from this moment. I don't believe in you or my father, and I am beginning to question what possible reason a merciful God could have for all this." She began to walk down the hall when Garrett pulled her back.

"Sorry. It doesn't work that way. I don't release you, Maggie. I don't release you to run away from me and hide in your bedroom. I don't release you to run away from dealing with your father and the pain that is firmly planted between you. And most of all," he spoke with determination, "I don't release you from a reconciliation with God." With that, Garrett turned and walked away.

Maggie stood openmouthed, looking after him. She was still standing there when Carmalita found her. Maggie waved her away. She needed to be alone.

What if Garrett was right? How could she learn to deal with all that stood between her and her father? Maggie suddenly remembered the Bible verse she'd found while on the train: " 'And he shall turn the heart of the fathers to the children, and the heart of the children to their fathers, lest I come and smite the earth with a curse.' "

Was God cursing her by taking Garrett Lucas away? What if something happened to Garrett and he died before being able to return to her? Would God curse her because she had been unwilling to put the past behind and open her heart to her father's love?

CHAPTER 13

July and August passed in a blur. Maggie's birthday came and went, and even though her father thoughtfully surprised her with gifts, Maggie barely acknowledged the day. Her heart ached. Garrett was gone.

Day after day, Jason approached his daughter, only to be waved off. Occasionally, Maggie had asked her father about Garrett's whereabouts, but Jason had promised not to tell her. His reward was his daughter's stubborn refusal to have anything to do with him. Jason refused to give up, however, and continued to find some small place in his daughter's life.

As September approached, Maggie's emotional state had not improved. She'd taken to riding Thunder every day. The huge Morgan crossbreed was aptly named. He was as black as midnight and stood fifteen hands high.

Everyone on the ranch murmured about

the Señor's sad-eyed daughter. Maggie spoke only to Carmalita and her father, and him, only when she had to.

As autumn flooded Piñon Canyon with golds and oranges, Jason began to worry. He wanted to make things right with Maggie before he died, but he couldn't reach through her pain and depression. Daily, he prayed for insight. His health was failing fast, and Jason feared if a reconciliation didn't take place soon, it might not take place at all.

On one particularly hot day, Maggie entered the courtyard where Jason was taking breakfast. She had grown extremely thin, and despite her golden tan from day after day in the sun, she didn't look well. Dark circles around her eyes gave her face a gaunt, inhuman look.

"Maggie, sit here with me," Jason commanded gently.

"I'm not hungry," Maggie said, pulling on her riding gloves. "I'm going to ride Thunder up on the ridge today."

"Maggie, I need you to sit for a moment with me. Surely you can give me . . ." Jason's words gave way to a fit of coughing. Maggie was painfully aware that the frequency of her father's coughing spells was increasing. The doctor had explained her father's lungs were filling with fluid and his heart couldn't work hard enough.

Maggie looked at her father's reddened face. As the coughing began to subside, she took the chair beside her father.

"Thank you, Maggie," Jason whispered. "Thank you for hearing me out."

Maggie said nothing. She allowed Carmalita to pour her some orange juice but waved away her offer of eggs and toast.

"Maggie, you need to take better care of yourself. You must eat. It isn't right." Maggie knew she had a problem. Carmalita had already taken in Maggie's clothes twice.

"Please don't worry," Maggie said. She didn't intend to grieve her father. She was only trying to forget the pain of losing Garrett.

"Maggie, I want you to listen to me. I know we can work this out, and I know you can come to love me again." Jason's voice broke, and Maggie ached at the thought of his pain.

She thought for a moment, then offered, "But I do love you, Father. I don't want you to worry. I do love you, and I know you love me." The words came mechanically and without feeling. It seemed a small price to offer the dying man.

"Maggie, love is so much more than

174

words. I want to spend time with you. I want to know your heart, and I want you to know mine. I have much to teach you about the ranch, and above everything else, I want you to come to know Jesus."

Maggie stiffened. God seemed to hammer her from every direction. Even when she rode Thunder and struggled to forget the image of Garrett's handsome, bearded face, God's words filled her mind. Maggie lowered her face, fearful of facing her father's eyes.

"I know you miss Garrett, I miss him too. He was my right hand, especially after I got sick," Jason continued. "I feel his absence daily, especially with winter coming on and the problems with the banditos in the hills." Jason hadn't intended to mention it to Maggie. He saw her eyes widen slightly.

"Bandits here?" Maggie questioned.

"It's possible. We've found some butchered cows, and several head are missing. It's unlikely that it's the Pueblos. I give them whatever they need through the mission." Maggie nodded.

"Maggie, I can't take back the past. God knows I would if it were possible. We both know, however, it's not." Jason struggled for air.

Maggie felt herself straining with every

breath. For the first time she noticed the purplish red color of her father's skin — skin that barely stretched over the bones of his face. Tears formed against Maggie's will.

"I don't know what to think anymore," she whispered. "I don't want to remember the pain of the past, and I don't understand why Garrett doesn't write. Why doesn't he let us know he's okay?" The words came out as whimpers, the fearful whimpers of a small child.

"I don't know, Maggie. I know we'd both feel better if he did, but I do know Garrett Lucas rides with God. Wherever he might be, God is by his side," Jason remarked confidently.

"If God rides with Garrett, maybe that's why He doesn't seem to be here," Maggie replied.

"God not here?" Jason exclaimed. "How can you say such a thing? God is all around us. He's urging your heart to listen. He is calling you to forgive and accept His forgiveness."

"Forgive?" Maggie questioned.

"Yes, forgive. I want you to forgive me for leaving you, Maggie. I want you to forgive me for shutting you out. Do you think it's possible?" Jason asked sincerely.

"I don't think it's a matter of forgiveness,

Father," Maggie began slowly. "I can't forget what happened. It changed so many things about me. It made me stronger, more independent, and I suppose more distant.

"I didn't make many friends. I feared they too, would leave me. When Garrett told me he was going, it was like watching it happen all over. I don't think it's a matter of forgiveness," Maggie said, lifting her eyes to face her father's surprised expression.

"But it is. Maggie, you haven't let go of the past. If you had forgiven me, you could have let Garrett go with his promise of return and believed him. You wouldn't be questioning your Heavenly Father, either."

Maggie thought over her father's words. Could they be true?

"I don't understand," Maggie finally said. "What does this have to do with God?"

"Maggie, your Heavenly Father is more reliable than your earthly one. You can count on God to be there every time, all the time, whenever you call out to Him. Don't harden your heart toward God. He isn't punishing you."

Her father's words seemed so clear, so truthful, yet Maggie hated to allow old feelings to surface. She hated to touch the emotions of the little girl from long ago, and she resented the fact she had to.

"If God loves me so much, why is He allowing me to hurt so badly?" Maggie couldn't hold back the tears. She put her face in her gloved hands and cried. "If God loves me, why did He take my mother and brother away?"

Jason was beside her in a moment, holding her and stroking her hair. There were tears in his eyes as well.

Eight years of pain and anguish poured from Maggie's heart. "He can't possibly love me. It isn't possible. I just know God hates me." Maggie's sobs tore at Jason's heart.

"Oh, Maggie, God does love you. As much as I love you, God loves you much more. We are like the silver and gold ore which runs through the rocks of the mountains. Precious and brilliant but useless without refining. We are being refined for God's purposes. I learned after your mother died that I had to accept God's will for my life and forgive."

Maggie lifted her face. "Forgive me?"

"No, Maggie," Jason whispered. "Forgive myself."

"What do you mean? You hadn't done anything wrong. I was the one who caught the fever, and all because I went to Lillie's house without permission." Maggie's sudden confession brought back her buried memories.

"Lillie's house!" Maggie whispered the words. Lillie's family had had the fever. Maggie remembered the red quarantine flag that had hung on the fence gate and front door of the Johnston house.

"I went to Lillie's house. Remember before Potwin Place, when we lived side by side in town?" Maggie questioned, painfully remembering details that she'd successfully repressed for years.

"I remember," Jason murmured.

"Mother was too busy to play with me. I was willful and spiteful, and I wanted to show her I could take care of myself. Mother told me to stay home. She explained the quarantine, but I didn't care.

"When she went to her room to rest, I went to Lillie's. I slipped in the back door, past their cook, and up the back stairs. Lillie wasn't as sick as her sisters, and I played with her. When I got sick the next day, I knew God hated me. Mother died because of me. She really did! Now I know why God is punishing me!" Maggie's body racked with uncontrollable sobs. "I killed my mother and brother!"

"No, Maggie! Listen to me," Jason said, pulling Maggie to her feet.

"It was all my fault, all my fault!" Maggie wailed hysterically.

It took all the strength Jason had to shake Maggie. "Stop it. Stop it, now! You did not kill your mother, but that mistaken idea has always stood between us, Maggie. Because of it, you thought I blamed you for her death." Maggie regained a bit of her composure, but tears still poured down her face.

"Well, didn't you? Even a little bit?"

"No, because I knew the truth," Jason said sadly.

"What truth?"

"We shared water from the same well as the Johnstons. Our well had caved in nearly three weeks earlier because of the flood. Remember? We had to stay with my mother because the Kaw River had flooded its banks. After the water receded and we returned home, I found that the well was beyond repair."

Maggie wiped her eyes. "I remember the flood. I remember all the mud we had to clean out of the house."

Jason smiled sadly. "You couldn't have caught typhoid overnight from a simple visit to Lillie. You were already exposed through the water we shared. Your mother was sick when you came down with the fever. It wasn't because of the baby that she couldn't continue to care for you through your illness. It was because she was sick herself. Don't you see, Maggie? She didn't get typhoid from you. She was already sick."

A tremendous weight lifted from Maggie's shoulders. "Then God didn't punish me for being disobedient by taking my mother and brother, and . . ." Maggie paused to study her father's face. "You!" she whispered softly.

"No, Maggie. God didn't punish you then, and He's not punishing you now. He's standing with open arms, just as I am."

"Oh, Father. I'm so sorry. Please forgive me!" Maggie threw her arms around her father's neck.

"Maggie, my Maggie, it is I who seek your forgiveness. Can you forgive me?"

"Oh, yes. A hundred times, yes!" They stood for several minutes holding each other. Jason's heart was filled with pure joy. His Maggie was home!

The remainder of the day passed much too quickly. Maggie listened to her father talk of his early days in New Mexico, trips to Colorado in search of gold and silver, and the ranch he'd created.

Maggie, in turn, tried to explain a lifetime of feelings and dreams. She was sharing a memory from her school days when Jason suggested a short walk in the rose garden.

Maggie linked her arm through Jason's and allowed his slow, faltering lead. "Please finish what you were saying," Jason encouraged.

Maggie started to speak, but just then he brought her to the garden. "It's beautiful!" she exclaimed. Her father had created a paradise. The rich, sweet fragrance of roses filled the air.

"How could I have lived here all this time and not known about this?" Maggie wondered aloud.

"Often we have precious things at our fingertips and fail to see them," Jason answered thoughtfully.

Maggie nodded and reached down to touch the velvet softness of a delicate yellow rose. "These are my favorites," she proclaimed, looking at the other roses as if to make certain.

Jason smiled proudly. "I've been experimenting with mixing varieties. This is one of my newer plants."

"What do you call it?"

"God's Hope."

Maggie stiffened slightly. "Father?"

"Yes?" Jason gave his daughter full attention.

"How can I be sure? About God, I mean.

How can I be sure I'm saved? Grandmother told me on many, many occasions, but it all seems so distant now."

Jason's heart soared. "It's very simple, Maggie. You ask God to forgive you and He does. You have to trust Him, Maggie. I know your trust doesn't come easily, but it's what faith is all about. Just repent and believe on the name of Jesus. He'll do the rest."

Later that night, Maggie knelt beside her bed for the first time in years.

"Heavenly Father, I know I am a willful and childish young woman. I know, too, that I am the one who's put walls between us. Thank you for letting me see this before it was too late. Please forgive me and help me to seek Your will in my life. I want Jesus to be my Savior, and I want to trust You all the days of my life. In Jesus' name I pray, amen."

As she got up, Maggie wondered, *Am I really saved?* She didn't feel different. Could she do as her father had suggested and trust God?

"If the Bible is true," Maggie said aloud, "and I believe it is, then I must trust. I need faith in God's ability to save me and to bring me new life through His Son. He's offered me a place to belong, but it's up to me to accept."

Maggie walked to the open French doors and looked out into the starlit sky. Garrett was out there somewhere. Would she ever see him again? He'd promised he'd be back for her, but could she believe him?

In the distance, coyotes yipped and howled at the moon. The echo of their mournful cries chilled Maggie.

"Please God," Maggie prayed aloud. "Please bring Garrett back to me."

CHAPTER 14

Garrett's mood was black and stormy. He stood beside his horse, Alder, using firm brush strokes to rid the animal's coat of clay and mud which had accumulated during their ride. It was the last day of September, and instead of giving routine orders to ready Piñon Canyon for the winter, Garrett was trapped twelve miles away at the mission David and Jenny Monroe had established for the Pueblos.

Alder sensed his master's mood and stood as still as stone. Garrett finished currying his horse, and after knocking most of the mud from his boots, he made his way to David and Jenny's house. The sky started to pour rain as Garrett entered the kitchen. Warmth hit his face in a welcome wave. The smell of tortillas and meat made him recognize how hungry he was.

"Garrett Lucas, you get in here and change those clothes!" Jenny Monroe demanded. Garrett smiled. Jenny was Garrett's junior by at least two or three years, but at times she seemed years older.

"Yes, Ma'am," Garrett drawled lazily and tipped his Stetson.

"Hurry up. Supper will be on shortly." It was all the encouragement Garrett needed.

An hour later, Garrett pushed away from the crude wood table and patted his stomach. "Good grub, Jenny!" he declared, and several little voices mimicked him.

"Good grub!"

Jenny Monroe looked down the twelve-foot table into the grateful brown eyes of the orphans she cared for.

"Go on with all of you," she said and stood to clear the table. She turned loving eyes to her husband of five years.

"David, why don't you and Garrett take yourselves to the sitting room, and I'll have Mary and Anna get these kids to bed." Seven little moans echoed down the length of the table, but the children who were old enough to take care of themselves got up from the table and raced upstairs. The older girls, Mary and Anna, tenderly cared for the youngest three.

"Come along, Garrett," David Monroe called. Garrett rose slowly from the table. He was tired and stiff from bringing down strays from the upper ranges.

The sitting room was warm and inviting. Garrett sat down in front of the fire, appreciating its warmth. He watched David Monroe put more wood on the fire. Garrett longed to hear of news from Piñon Canyon, but he waited patiently for David to sit.

"I suppose you'd like to hear the latest," David said, joining Garrett in a chair by the fire.

"You know I would. It was all I could do to wait through dinner. How's Maggie?" Garrett asked anxiously.

"I have a letter. Would you like to read it?" David asked, pulling the envelope from his pocket. Garrett nearly leaped from the chair to take the precious paper from his friend. He scanned the pages with intense interest. At one point David thought he saw tears in Garrett's eyes, but just as quickly his eyes dried.

"She's accepted the past. That's good," Garrett said absently. "And she's accepted Jesus as her Savior. That's even better!" Joy surged through Garrett's heart. Maggie was working through the past with her father, and soon, very soon, he could return to the ranch and marry her.

"David, this is wonderful news! Why didn't you tell me sooner?"

David Monroe chuckled. "Easy, Garrett. There's still a long way to go."

"I know all that, but it's a huge step forward. I mean, if you'd seen her these last few months. She's skin and bones, and the dangerous way she rode the gelding made me want to give up at least a thousand times."

"I told you it wasn't wise to spy on her," David reminded.

"I know, but I couldn't help it. I just had to feel close to her. I've loved her for so long."

David nodded. "I know what you mean. It was a good thing Jenny lived in the same town as the Bible college I attended. I would have gone mad without her."

"Then you understand," Garrett whispered. "David, sometimes, I'm not sure what to make of it. At first I thought it was a silly infatuation. But as I listened to the letters from her grandmother, I drank in every word about Maggie and couldn't wait to meet her," Garrett paused, remembering his anticipation of their first meeting.

"When I finally stood outside her house in Potwin, I wasn't sure I could play my part. I'd already told Jason how I felt, and he couldn't have been happier. But I knew I'd need to convince Maggie, and I wasn't

188

sure I could. Boy, the prayer that went into that one!"

David smiled. "I always believed God was setting you up for something special, Garrett."

"He sure was. When I realized that Maggie was falling for me, I started to panic. There was the matter of her father, and I was even more troubled by the wall she'd built to shut out God. She couldn't see God's love for her. That's why this letter offers the best possible news. Maggie has learned she can count on God."

The two men barely heard the rustling of Jenny's skirts as she brought coffee into the sitting room.

"Here we are," she said in her soft, gentle voice. Garrett had heard that voice comfort heartbroken children and soothe the worried heart of her husband. Jenny Monroe's every action reflected her Savior.

"Thank you, Jenny," Garrett said as he took the offered cup. "David just showed me the letter. Isn't it great news?"

"It certainly is, Garrett. Just what we've prayed for. We must continue to pray, however. You know how hard this time will be." Jenny spoke with authority. Garrett wondered if something in her past gave her special insight.

"I reckon it will be at that," Garrett replied. Truth was, he hadn't considered anything past the contents of the letter.

"I think it would be a good time to drop a note of encouragement, Garrett," David interjected.

"Oh, yes," Jenny agreed, sitting next to her husband. They exchanged a look of tenderness which made Garrett's heart ache.

"You think so?" Garrett asked hopefully. He'd wanted to write Maggie every day, but at the advice of David and Jenny, he'd given Maggie the opportunity to make the right choices on her own.

"Definitely," David began. "She'll need to know you still care, and she'll need to know you've been praying for her — you're still praying for her. Maybe," David added, remembering something Garrett had said earlier, "maybe you should let her know you've never been far away, that you've been watching over her."

"I think that'd be nice, Garrett," Jenny said. "I know a woman's heart likes to hear things like that. Share some encouraging Scripture too. She'll need the Word as she learns to walk in faith."

Garrett got to his feet, nearly spilling his coffee. "I'll do it right now. Do you suppose

Lupe could deliver it tomorrow?"

"I'm sure he'd be happy to," David said enthusiastically. "I've got some papers to send to Jason anyway, so the trip will be necessary for both of us."

Jenny placed her hand upon her husband's cheek. "Why don't we leave Garrett to his letter? I would love an evening stroll." The love shone clear in her eyes, and David wrapped an arm around her and pulled her close.

"I'd like that too," he agreed. "If you'll excuse us," David said, rising to his feet. "We have a walk to take."

Garrett watched as they left the room. David and Jenny Monroe shared a deep, abiding love. Garrett dreamed of a love like that with Maggie, and the news he'd just received finally made it possible.

Later that night, after pouring his heart onto three pages of David's personal stationery, Garrett lay in bed staring up at the ceiling. "How much longer, Lord?" he wondered aloud. "How much longer until I can go home?"

He thought about the words he'd written. He'd wanted to explain everything he felt. He kept remembering how Maggie had told him she wouldn't wait for him. How would she feel now that she'd made peace with

God and her father?

Long into the night, Garrett tossed and turned. His sleep was fitful, and more than once he woke up drenched in sweat. Morning couldn't come too soon.

Back at Piñon Canyon, Maggie awoke to the warmth of fall sunshine. She stretched slowly and purposefully like a sleek mountain puma.

For a moment, Maggie listened to the morning sounds of the ranch. She smiled at the smell of hot coffee and bacon. Maria was preparing breakfast. After months of near starvation, Maggie felt like making up for lost time.

Quickly, she threw back the covers and went to her vanity. She poured cool water from the pitcher and washed the sleep from her face. Carmalita hadn't arrived to help her dress, but Maggie didn't mind. She went to the wardrobe and pulled out a dusty rose day dress. Just as Maggie was securing the last few buttons, Carmalita knocked and entered the room.

"Señorita Maggie, you should have called for me," Carmalita said, rushing to help Maggie.

"Nonsense. I'm not an invalid, even if I've acted like a sick cow for the last few months." Carmalita looked shocked, and Maggie gave a little laugh. "I'm sorry, Carmalita. I'm really not loco, as Maria would call it. I've finally found peace."

Carmalita began to brush Maggie's thick, auburn hair as Maggie continued to explain. "These past months, I died a little each day, wondering if my harsh words had driven away the man I hoped to marry. I hated myself for hurting my father and for being so ungrateful. But you know, Carmalita," Maggie said, pausing to put her thoughts in just the right words. "The worst part was my alienation from God."

"What do you mean?" Carmalita questioned.

Maggie took hold of Carmalita's hands. "Carmalita, two days ago I gave my heart to Jesus. I'm at peace with God, and now I can truly begin to live."

Carmalita smiled shyly, but with understanding. "That is good, Señorita Maggie. I, too, am a Christian."

"You are!" Maggie exclaimed with positive delight. "How wonderful. We can help each other."

Carmalita seemed happy with the change in her mistress. She finished Maggie's hair quickly and went to tidy up the room.

Maggie whirled in front of the mirror, suddenly very interested in how she looked. The rose colored dress hugged her slim figure, and the gored skirt swept out from her hips and flowed to the floor. The wine trim on the bodice and sleeves made her hair look a deeper, coppery color. Satisfied with her appearance, Maggie joined her father for breakfast.

"My, you're up early, aren't you?" Jason said as Maggie took her place at the table. "And don't you look pretty."

"Thank you, Father."

Maria placed platters of fried potatoes, scrambled eggs, and ham on the table. Maggie helped herself to generous portions of everything.

"What would you like to do today?" Maggie asked her father between bites.

"I'm afraid I'm not up to a great deal." Jason gave a series of hoarse coughs which left him breathless.

"What if we enjoy each other's company here in the house? You can tell me more stories about the years we've missed, and I can tell you some of mine." Maggie tried to hide her concern for her father, but it was evident by the furrow of her brow.

"You mustn't worry, Maggie. I don't fear death. I have found peace with God and with my beloved daughter. I can go home to heaven with a peace I'd only dreamed possible."

"I wish you wouldn't talk about dying, Father. It seems like asking for trouble." Maggie sounded tense and curt. She hated her father referring to his death. She wasn't ready to let go of him.

"Maggie, you can't pretend something isn't going to happen just because you don't like the idea," Jason sighed. "I wish I could stay to see you married and with children of your own. I'd like to watch you and Garrett take over the running of this ranch. But I only asked God to let me live long enough for us to put our differences aside. He's given me that and more. I'd say anything else is added blessings."

"But, Father." Maggie started to protest, but Jason waved his hand.

"Don't blame God or resent His timing. Promise me, Maggie. Promise me you won't allow my death to cause bitterness in your heart."

Maggie looked at her father for a moment. His faded blue eyes were sunk deep into his face. There was a grayish pallor to his skin and frailty to his movements.

"How can I promise a thing like that? I don't want to lose you. It seems like I just found you, and now you'll be taken from me." Maggie said thoughtfully.

"You must trust God, Maggie. In His infinite wisdom, He will work all things together for good. Would you have me stay and suffer like this?"

"No, Father. Never! I didn't mean —"

"I know you never meant it that way," Jason said, taking hold of Maggie's hand. "But you must consider my viewpoint. I'm tired of the weakness, the lack of air, the coughing. It pains me to remember the man I used to be and to see the man I've become."

Her father was right, Maggie realized. It was pure selfishness to want her father to continue living. And for what? Her pleasure? Her need?

"Forgive me, Father. I want the very best for you, and I promise I won't hate God for whatever the best may be. If it means losing you soon, and I pray it doesn't, then I will accept His will. In the meantime, I want to enjoy every moment." Maggie gave her father's hand a squeeze.

"Good. You have no way of knowing the contentment that gives me."

Maggie smiled and felt at peace. She finally had the father she'd longed for, and with him came the security of belonging.

CHAPTER 15

Before Garrett's letter could be delivered by Lupe, another letter arrived at Piñon Canyon. With it came the news that Sophia Intissar had passed away.

Devastated, Maggie sat in front of the fireplace, watching the dying embers of a late morning fire. Her heart ached and her throat felt painfully tight. She wanted to cry, but the tears wouldn't come.

Maggie couldn't forget the anguished look on her father's face when he'd read the news. Her father had collapsed on the nearest chair and cried bitter, pain-filled tears. When her father's emotions had sent him into paroxysms of coughing, Maggie had called for Miguel to help him to bed. Medication had finally brought her father the relief of sleep.

Several hours had passed, and Maggie couldn't believe how quiet the house had grown. Usually the muffled sounds of Maria singing in the kitchen or Carmalita talking excitedly about her upcoming wedding to Miguel filled the house.

Maggie lifted the letter again. It had been penned more than a week earlier by Lillie Johnston Philips. Lillie had always loved Sophia as her own grandmother. She told Maggie that Sophia had died peacefully in her sleep. Lillie, nearly four months a bride, had helped her parents arrange for the burial services, despite the fact she had discovered she was in a family way.

Maggie smiled at Lillie's reference to the new life she carried. One life ended and another began. And in her father's bedroom, still another life hung in the balance.

Maggie noted that her grandmother had been buried the same day she and her father had resolved their differences. Perhaps her grandmother had sensed an end to the painful past and knew she could go to heaven unhampered by regrets and worries. Maggie smiled at the thought of her grandmother walking the streets of heaven and enjoying the company of many old friends.

"Heavenly Father," Maggie prayed. "I thank You for the years I shared with Grandmother. I'll miss her very much, but I know she's safe and happy, and for now, that seems enough. Please be with Father. He isn't strong enough to bear much more, and I'm not ready to let go of him. Help me to prepare for his passing, and please don't let him suffer. In Jesus' name, amen." When she finished praying, Maggie felt a great peace that gave her the strength to go on.

Later that afternoon, another letter was placed in Maggie's hands. Even though she had never seen Garrett's handwriting before, she knew the letter was from him. Retreating to the privacy of her bedroom, she tore open the envelope. Her heart beat faster as she read his greeting.

My beloved Maggie,
    A tremendous burden has been lifted. I was just told of your reconciliation with Jason, and your acceptance of Jesus as Savior. I want to shout for joy. I know how you have struggled with God over the years. I know it was never easy to see God as the loving Father He is. Now, however, I desire more than ever to share my life with you and grow together in the love He has given us.

The letter continued, and Maggie drank in each word. Every sentence was exactly what she'd longed to hear. She read Garrett's words of love and pledges of lifelong devotion. How it thrilled her to see each cherished promise and know without doubt that he loved her. Maggie's one disappointment was Garrett didn't give a specific time when he would return. She folded the letter and tucked it into her skirt pocket to read again later.

Even though it was the beginning of October and the afternoons no longer held the intense heat of summer, Maggie had grown accustomed to siesta. After checking on her father, she decided to stretch out and take a nap.

Nearly two hours later, Carmalita urgently woke Maggie.

"Maggie, Maggie! Come quickly. Your father is very ill." The fear in Carmalita's voice left Maggie shaken. She ran after Carmalita to where Jason Intissar lay vomiting blood.

"Carmalita, what are we going to do?" Maggie cried. She held her father's bony shoulders steady as another spell of coughing began.

"We can send Miguel for the doctor," Carmalita offered.

"Then do it, and tell him to go quickly!" Maggie exclaimed. "And Carmalita . . ."

"Sí?" Carmalita answered, pausing in the doorway.

"You'd better get a couple of ranch hands — men my father is fond of. I'm going to need help until Miguel and the doctor get here."

"Right away," Carmalita replied and quickly left the room.

Maggie turned her attention back to her father. "Father, is the cough passing?"

"I think so. Let me lay back on the pillows." Jason's voice was barely audible.

Maggie eased her father back. Her father seemed oblivious to any comfort the new position offered. He strained for each breath, and Maggie fought the urge to run from the room.

To get her mind off her father's ragged breathing, Maggie began cleaning up the area around his bed. Carmalita returned and took over the cleaning, urging Maggie to care for her father.

Maggie sat stroking her father's balding head. She dipped a cloth in cool water and began to wipe away blood stains from his face.

"We came as quick as we could, Ma'am."

Maggie looked up to find the compassionate eyes of Bill, her father's trusted foreman. Behind him stood a young man she'd never met.

"This here is Mack's little brother, Rob,"

Bill explained. Maggie offered a brief smile to the shy, sandy-haired young man.

"Thank you both for coming. Father's been taken by quite a bad spell this time. I sent Miguel for the doctor, but I know I'll need help with him before they return," she whispered. Her father's labored breathing became even louder, and Maggie could barely concentrate on what she was saying.

"No problem, Ma'am. I'd give my life for Mr. Jason. He's been a right good boss and friend," Bill said, lowering his eyes to the dusty hem of his jeans. Rob remained silent.

"Bill, I think Father would rest better if we could prop him up. I can't lift him, but if you and Rob could help me, we might get the job done."

"Sure thing, Miss Maggie." Bill's voice held the devoted enthusiasm Maggie needed to hear. Together, the three worked to ease Jason into a more comfortable position.

The hours wore on, and Maggie felt encouraged as her father's breathing became less ragged. She dozed in a chair, and only when the clock chimed midnight did she agree to turn in.

Maggie started to slip into bed fully clothed. There seemed little sense in undressing. What if her father grew suddenly worse? Carmalita would hear nothing of it.

"No one will care if you appear at your father's beside in your robe. But you need your rest," Carmalita said, taking charge of Maggie as if she were a child.

"But," Maggie started to protest.

"You'll sleep much better in your nightgown, and you'll need all your strength." Carmalita finished pulling Maggie's blood-stained dress over her head and replaced it with a fresh cotton nightgown.

"I'll have Bill wake me if your father wakes up or gets any worse." Carmalita said, blowing out the candle. Maggie wanted to argue, but her mind wouldn't make sense of the situation. Reluctantly, she fell back against her pillow and slept.

The first crimson rays of the late fall sun were peeking over the mountaintops when Maggie woke with a start. Remembering her father, she threw back the covers, pulled on her robe, and raced down the hallway.

When she opened the door, Maggie was surprised to find Dr. Avery leaning over her father. He looked up as Maggie entered the room.

"Good morning, Miss Intissar," he said in his deep, rumbling voice. "I've been here for about an hour."

"I wanted to check . . . I mean, how is

he?" Maggie asked in a nervous whisper.

"He's sleeping. I've given him morphine," Dr. Avery informed her.

"Morphine? What's that?" Maggie asked. Finding her courage, she drew closer to her father's bed.

"It's a drug that will take your father's pain away and help him to sleep. Your father is a very sick man, Miss Intissar, but of course you know this."

"Yes, I do. I want the truth, though. Is he going to die? I mean right away, today?" Maggie's voice betrayed the pain of her heart.

"I can't be certain, but I don't look for him to leave this bed again," Dr. Avery said with finality. Maggie's knees weakened. Her face turned ashen as the meaning of the doctor's words sank in.

"I'm sorry, Miss Intissar," the doctor said, helping Maggie to a chair. "You must be strong. You'll not be any good to him this way."

"I know," Maggie whispered. "But it seems so unfair. I just found him, and now I will lose him once more." Dr. Avery turned back to his medical bag.

"I am going to leave enough morphine powder so you can give it to him regularly. He won't be in his right mind while on the medicine, but he won't hurt either," the doctor explained matter-of-factly. "Should I instruct Maria about the dosing?"

"Please, that would be best," Maggie said, recognizing that she herself wouldn't remember any instructions.

"I'll be leaving, then. There's nothing more I can do. I've been with your father through the thick and thin of this illness. We both knew it would come to this. I must tell you, Miss Intissar, your father has faced his illness bravely, always insisting on the truth no matter how bad the news. He's been a good friend, and I will miss him sorely when he's gone." Dr. Avery's rock solid voice broke.

Tears fell unbidden down Maggie's cheeks. What a beautiful memorial to the man who lay dying. "Thank you, Dr. Avery. Thank you for being his friend, and thank you for coming to care for him once more. I'll let you know when it's over." Maggie got to her feet. "Forgive me for not walking with you to the kitchen, but I want to stay with my father."

"I understand, Miss Intissar," Dr. Avery said, turning to leave. "If it's any comfort," he added, "your father won't know what's happening. He won't feel the pain, and he won't strain to breathe."

Maggie gently stroked her father's icy hand. "Thank you. Thank you so much."

CHAPTER 16

A few days later, Maggie was presented with a problem she'd not anticipated. Bill informed her that the regular supply trip hadn't been made to finish stocking up for the winter.

"I know it's late notice, Ma'am. We should've thought of it a lot sooner, but what with your pa so sick and all, it just slipped my mind," Bill offered apologetically.

"I understand, Bill. I'm just not sure what we should do about it. I don't know anything about running this ranch. My father wanted me to learn and we had great plans, but now it's apparently not to be," Maggie said sadly.

"We've been lucky so far. The snows have stayed put, and we've enjoyed mild weather. But I think it's about to end. My joints have been bothering me somethin' fierce, and that always means a change in the weather,"

Bill said, rubbing his elbow.

"What should we do?" Maggie asked earnestly. Just then, Carmalita entered the room with hot mugs of coffee.

"Maria thought you'd enjoy this Mexican coffee."

"Mexican coffee?" Maggie questioned, sniffing the contents of her mug.

"Sí, it has cinnamon in it," Carmalita said with a smile. Carmalita smiled a great deal these days because she planned to marry Miguel shortly before Christmas.

"How interesting," Maggie murmured and sipped the coffee. "It's delicious." She cast a bittersweet smile at the dark-eyed servant. Maggie longed for a wedding of her own.

"Maria's Mexican coffee warms a fellow's bones and treats the tongue to a feast," Bill said with enthusiasm.

"Well, I'm afraid despite the good coffee, we still have a big problem. Bill, do you know anything about the book running of the ranch?" Maggie asked the bewildered foreman.

"Not a thing, Miss Maggie. Never had to. Your pa always left it to Garrett, that is, when he didn't take care of it himself."

Maggie sighed. "I wish we had Garrett with us now. I'd gladly let him take over everything."

"I could have Miguel ride out after him," Carmalita suggested.

"What?" Maggie's voice clearly showed her surprise. "You know where Garrett is?"

"Sí," Carmalita answered matter-of-factly. "Your father has kept in touch with him at the Pueblo mission."

"That's our answer, Miss Maggie. If we can get Garrett here, we'll be fixed fine. He'll be knowin' just what to do and when," Bill remarked, handing his mug back to Carmalita. "Now if you'll excuse me, I've got some ranch hands to see to."

"Thank you, Bill. I'll have Miguel go after Garrett immediately," Maggie called out to the retreating figure. She turned to Carmalita. "Send Miguel right away. Have him tell Garrett everything."

"Sí," Carmalita replied and rushed off to locate Miguel.

Maggie went to check on her father. She could hardly contain her excitement. Garrett would be coming home. She smiled to herself. It had been over three months since Garrett had walked out of her life. Even so, Maggie remembered his promise to make her his wife. A shiver ran through her. *Garrett's wife!*

Jason Intissar slept peacefully. The morphine had made him oblivious to every-thing, but at least he didn't hurt. For that Maggie was grateful.

Absentmindedly, she picked up some knitting she'd left beside her father's bed. It was to be a blanket for Lillie's baby. The thought of her young friend newly married and expecting her first child brought tears to Maggie's eyes. She remembered leaving the note for Lillie before she left Topeka and promising to return in time for the wedding.

Maggie smiled at the memory of the smug, spoiled girl she had been. Spoiled. It was what Garrett had called her, and he'd been quite accurate.

Maggie worked on the blanket and thought of what their meeting would be like. Would she be sitting down to dinner when Garrett came rushing through the door? Perhaps he wouldn't make it until morning. Maggie's mind raced with thoughts. Would he see the change in her, or would he still believe her to be a spoiled child?

Carmalita came in to tend the fire. The late autumn days had grown chilly, and while the adobe ranch house was well insulated with its thick walls, there was an undeniable hint of winter in the air. Bill's joints must have been right about the change in weather.

"Did you send Miguel?" Maggie asked anxiously.

"Sí, he was happy to go. He has missed Señor Lucas, but more I think he wanted to talk to Pastor Monroe. He will marry us," Carmalita replied as she stoked the fire. The wood she added to the cherry red coals ignited immediately, warming the room.

"Are you finished with your wedding dress yet?" Maggie inquired, caught up in Carmalita's excitement.

"Not quite," the girl answered. She went around the room, tidying up anything that seemed out of place.

"Do you need anything else to complete it?" Maggie questioned, thinking she could go with Garrett to get supplies.

"No, I have everything. It's just the waiting that's hard." Maggie nodded in heartfelt agreement with Carmalita's words.

The day stretched into evening, and when Maggie found her legs cramped from hours of sitting, she decided to take a walk. The liquid gold sun dripped lazily between two snow-covered peaks. Golds, pinks, purples, and oranges swirled delicate fingers against the cold gray-blue of the evening sky. It was breathtaking!

Maggie wandered to the corral where

Thunder stood stomping at the dirt. He wanted to run as much as Maggie wished to ride. As she approached, he whinnied softly and came to greet her. His nudging muzzle was disappointed to find Maggie's cupped hand held no surprise of sugar or carrots.

"Sorry, Boy. Not this time." Maggie watched the sleek gelding move away to seek out food. She loved him. She loved almost everything about Piñon Canyon Ranch. Strange that she had fought coming here. It was somewhat like coming home. No, it was more. She had come home.

As Maggie walked slowly back to the house, her thoughts again drifted to Garrett. She looked up to the mountains and wondered if he could see her now. But the mountains surrounding Piñon Canyon refused to give up any secrets.

Supper was quiet and lonely. Maggie's slim frame was only starting to fill out again. Carmalita was always trying to get her to eat. Many times, Maria sent tempting treats from the kitchen for "Señor's skinny daughter," as Maria teasingly called Maggie.

Maggie picked at her meal. It wasn't a lack of hunger that kept her pushing the food from one side of the plate to the other. It was the memory of Garrett. Everywhere she looked, she saw laughing blue eyes, and when she was least expecting it, the wind carried the sweet musky scent of his cologne.

Maggie finally gave up on the roasted chicken and went to the library. Carmalita had thoughtfully started a fire in the library's wood stove, and the room beckoned to Maggie. She loved the library.

Maggie picked up a book she'd been trying to read since her father had fallen ill. The book still held little interest, however, and Maggie placed it back on the shelf.

She went to the huge walnut desk that commanded the attention of anyone who entered the room. Her father had ordered the desk made to fit his specifications. Solid walnut, it had been varnished slightly to bring out the dark lines of the wood's natural grain. It was trimmed with brass handles for the four drawers which lined either side and with brass corner plates at the top edges of the desk.

Maggie sat down in the black leather chair she'd seen her father work from. It swallowed her up. Lovingly, Maggie touched the desktop and its contents. These were the papers her father had been working on before becoming ill. How she wished she understood the running of the ranch books.

She'd see to it that Garrett taught her all about them. It seemed very important to know every detail of the ranch — how it was run, when they performed certain duties, and why.

Maggie reluctantly made the familiar walk down the long hall to her father's bedroom. Bill was preparing to bed down on the small cot at the foot of the bed. Maggie glanced at the clock on the fireplace mantel, surprised to see it was nearly ten o'clock.

Confident her father was sleeping soundly, Maggie found Carmalita and informed her she was going to bed. Bill would notify them if anything needed their attention.

Maggie smiled when she discovered Carmalita had already prepared a fire in Maggie's bedroom. Maggie warmed herself for a moment, then slipped into a nightgown. She was about to get into bed when she heard a knock at the door. It was Carmalita.

"Come quickly, Maggie. Señor is not good."

Maggie threw on her robe and raced down the hall after Carmalita. Nothing could have prepared Maggie for the sight of her father writhing and crying out in agony. How could this be? Moments ago, he'd rested comfortably.

"What happened, Bill?" Maggie cried as

she rushed to her father's side.

"I don't rightly know, Miss Maggie," Bill began. "I was just getting to sleep when he started a thrashin' and moanin'. I'm afeared the medicine ain't doin' its job."

"That doesn't make any sense. We gave him the regular dosage. It's always worked before," Maggie stated in utter confusion. How could she stop her father's intense pain?

"Father, it's Maggie."

For a moment, the older man's eyes opened. They seemed to flash recognition, then they rolled back, their heavy lids closed. Maggie's tears burned hot on her cheeks. *Dear God, how much more can he stand? Why is he allowed to suffer like this?*

Maria arrived with a larger dose of medication, and after Bill, Maggie, and Carmalita were able to hold Jason's thrashing body still, Maria forced the medicine down his throat.

Maggie sat for the next two hours, waiting as her father's pain faded into peaceful sleep. She dozed off and on, and when Bill suggested she make her way back to bed, she didn't argue.

Gratefully, Maggie climbed once again into the warmth and comfort of her own bed. Her eyes refused to stay open, and her mind was clouded with sleep. Her last clear thought was to wonder what was keeping Garrett and Miguel.

CHAPTER 17

When Garrett and Miguel hadn't shown up by the end of the second day, both Carmalita and Maggie began to worry.

"They should have been here by now," Maggie said, pulling back the curtain and searching for any sign of the two men.

"Sí," Carmalita said softly as she cleared the breakfast dishes.

As the day warmed to an unseasonable temperature, Maggie determined to ride out on Thunder in hopes of meeting the men as they returned. Even Carmalita agreed it was a good plan.

Maggie checked in on her father first. He slept soundly, and Maria was keeping careful watch for any signs of discomfort. There was little need to worry about the addictive effects of the medication. It was clear to everyone that Jason Intissar would soon join his wife in heaven.

Maggie slipped into a dark blue riding

skirt. She pulled on her long boots. They almost felt foreign to her. It had been over a week since she'd ridden. She finished dressing and tied her auburn hair at the nape of her neck with a ribbon.

Making her way to the corral, Maggie located Bill and coaxed him into saddling Thunder for her. Bill had been an absolute lifesaver, and Maggie intended to thank him properly when things settled down.

Although Maggie had never been to the mission, she'd paid careful attention to Bill's directions and landmarks. She didn't intend to go very far, but by midday, she'd covered quite a bit of ground. The sun was blazing overhead.

Maggie paused to take a drink from her canteen, grateful that Bill had insisted on her taking it. Thunder whinnied softly.

"It's okay, Boy," Maggie said, recognizing her mount's thirst. "If Bill's directions are right, a water hole lies just ahead."

As Maggie neared the water hole, a hideous odor filled the air. The stench grew unbearable as Maggie approached the water. She could see strange mounds of dirt on the far side of the hole, but as she drew near, Maggie realized they weren't mounds of dirt at all. The ground was littered with partially butchered cattle carcasses.

Maggie felt nauseated, and Thunder whinnied nervously at the sight. The bloated carcasses were not only beside the water hole, but in the water itself, hopelessly fouling the contents for human or animal use.

Maggie's mind whirled. What could it mean? She'd heard the hands speak of rustlers in the area, and there was the ever-present worry of banditos. The renegade band of Mexicans, Indians, and mixed breeds were a constant worry to the outlying ranches. Banditos had families hidden high in the rocky hills, and they were considered a brotherhood of the utmost secrecy.

Maggie knew Maria had family among the banditos, although she never spoke of it to Maggie. Carmalita had whispered the secret to Maggie, telling her it was one reason Piñon Canyon suffered no more loss than an occasional steer.

Surveying the carnage and waste, Maggie grew cold. She pulled Thunder's reins hard and put him into a full gallop. She wanted to get back home, and she pressed Thunder to the limit of his endurance, fully aware of the white foam which spotted the gelding's coat.

After covering half the distance to the ranch, Maggie remembered Thunder's need for water. She reined the huge gelding to a stop and dismounted. Pouring the contents of her canteen into her hat, she placed it under Thunder's nuzzle. Thunder greedily lapped up the water. It seemed such an inadequate offering, but Maggie had no other choice.

Silently, she surveyed the land around her. It was rocky and dry. Climbing back into her well-worn saddle, Maggie felt uncomfortable. Once again she looked around her. The mountains rose majestically, and their snow-capped peaks shown as brilliant halos against the intense blue of the sky. Nothing here should make her uneasy, but remembering the water hole, Maggie decided things weren't as innocent as they appeared. Cautiously, she made her way back to the ranch.

The sun was starting down when Maggie rode into the corral yard. Bill was frantic.

"Where've ya been? I've been worried sick, feared that maybe those banditos got hold of ya. I should'a never let ya go," Bill ranted as he helped Maggie dismount.

"I'm fine, Bill. Really," Maggie said.

"Then what's that tone of voice about?" Bill questioned as he handed Thunder's reins to one of Maria's sons.

"Bill," Maggie began as soon as the boy

was out of earshot. "I found some dead steers at the first water hole."

"What'd ya say?" Bill asked, uncertain his ears had heard right. Maggie started walking toward the house, and Bill realized she meant for him to follow.

"I don't want anyone to overhear me," Maggie offered as a brief explanation. She paused as they neared the house. "I found seven or eight partially butchered steers. They are all around the water hole and some were even dumped in the water itself."

"Banditos!" Bill exclaimed.

"Do you think so?" Maggie asked, feeling sick again as she remembered the sight at the water hole.

"Has to be. Rustlers wouldn't butcher 'em. They'd drive 'em off and sell them. Banditos can't drive the steers up into their hideouts, so they take what they want or need and leave the carcasses."

"If it is banditos, what will they do next?" Maggie wondered aloud.

"Probably nothing right now," Bill answered deep in thought.

"Bill, we've got to get to Garrett and Miguel. Is there someone else we can send to the mission?" Maggie questioned. "I — we need him so much right now," she added, desperation mounting.

"I'll get Mack. If I send him in the morning, they should be back by nightfall." Bill's words offered little comfort, but when the older man's large, weatherworn hand came down on Maggie's, warmth and closeness briefly stilled her fears.

The following morning, Maggie and Bill stood in the yard watching Mack ride away. Maggie offered a silent prayer for Mack's safety and speed. As she turned to go to the house, she noticed Bill's hesitant steps.

"Maybe we should'a sent someone with him," Bill muttered, and Maggie wondered if he was right. Neither one said another word. Maggie nodded slightly, and Bill touched the brim of his dirty white hat as they parted for their respective duties.

The day moved in slow motion. The only positive bit of excitement was her father. Maggie entered the sickroom to find Maria talking in low whispers to her father.

"Father, but how? Oh, Maria. I thought I'd never be able to talk to him again," Maggie cried as she knelt beside the bed of her father. His slightly drugged gaze fell on his daughter.

"Your papa is doing much better," Maria explained, "so I lessened his medication."

"You aren't hurting?" Maggie questioned, taking hold of her father's hand and holding it to her cheek.

"No, not as much." Jason barely whispered the words.

Maggie breathed a sigh of relief. "Father, there is so much I need to talk to you about. I need you so much." Maggie let her tears fall unashamed against her father's hand.

"Don't cry," Jason murmured and, using all his strength, he gave Maggie's hand a slight squeeze.

"Father, I can't lose you now. Please get well," Maggie begged.

Jason shook his head. His eyes were nearly lifeless. Maggie could see the pallor had not changed, and every breath her father drew brought a hideous rattling sound. A death rattle, Maria had called it.

Maggie straightened her shoulders. It was enough that she could share a few more words of endearment. It was enough that she could tell her father of her love one more time. Peace settled over her, and Maggie decided against telling her father about the ranch's needs and Miguel's absence.

"I love you, Papa," Maggie said, smoothing his forehead.

"I love you too," Jason breathed weakly.

"I'm glad you made me come here. I'm thankful to God that you sent Garrett for me. I know it was right for me to put the past behind and to accept your forgiveness and God's." Jason said nothing, but the slight upturning of his mouth told Maggie he was pleased.

Maggie continued to talk even as Jason dozed and the shadows of afternoon fell across the room. The room chilled. Maggie placed a few pieces of kindling in the fireplace and watched with satisfaction as the wood ignited. The room grew comfortable again, and Maggie was just settling down beside her father's bed when Carmalita came in to light the lamps. The worried look on her face reflected the torture she felt at Miguel's absence.

"Don't worry, Carmalita. They'll all be back soon." Maggie tried to offer the words as an encouragement, but Carmalita rushed out of the room sobbing. Maggie started to go after her, but her father's weak voice stopped her.

"Who'll be back, Maggie?"

"Oh Father, don't worry about it. Everything is fine, really it is," Maggie said soothingly. She didn't want her father to worry.

"Where's Garrett? I'd like to see him, Maggie." Jason said, seeming to forget his concern.

"I've sent for him, Father. He'll be here soon."

"You do love him, don't you? I wouldn't force you to marry him. You know that, don't you?" His words required great effort.

"I know, Father. I know," Maggie assured her father.

"You didn't answer me," Jason whispered and coughed. Maggie feared the cough would return and sought to quiet her father.

"Hush now, Father. Please relax or you'll spend all your energy." Maggie gently stroked her father's hand, hoping to quiet him.

"Maggie," Jason struggled to speak. "I . . . have to . . . know." He was gasping for breath and Maggie wondered if she should find Maria. She stood as if to go, but Jason refused to release her hand. "I have to know," he said more firmly.

"Know what, Father?" Maggie asked, confused by her father's sudden strength.

"I have to know if you love him. Do you love Garrett Lucas, as a woman should love a man who'll be her husband?" Jason's eyes were suddenly clear, and Maggie knew he was studying her intently. Perhaps he couldn't die in peace without knowing she'd be happy.

Maggie fell to her knees beside the bed. "Yes, Father. I love Garrett very much. I think I've loved him since I first laid eyes on him in our parlor back in Potwin. If not then, I'm sure I fell in love with him when he caught me in his arms as I was trying to escape down the trellis." It was the first time Maggie had admitted to herself when her love for Garrett had taken root.

Carmalita reentered the room, but Maggie continued to talk unashamedly of her love for Garrett. "Father, you were so wise in choosing such a man for me. I'm sorry I was such a willful and spoiled child. Garrett called me that, you know? Willful and spoiled," Maggie remembered with a laugh. "I was too." A sudden thought caused Maggie to worry, and her concern was reflected on her face.

"What is it, Maggie? There's something more you aren't telling me." Jason's look of alarm caused Maggie to share her fears aloud.

"It's only that I told Garrett to stay away. I told him I wouldn't wait for him. I wasn't very nice, Father."

"Is that all?" Jason sounded relieved. The sudden smile on his face confused Maggie all the more.

"Is that all? Isn't that enough? I love him," Maggie said, lowering her eyes. "What if he doesn't love me anymore?"

Maggie felt firm hands on her shoulders,

and Garrett's deep voice stilled all her fears. "There's no chance of that, Maggie Intissar. I will always love you."

"Garrett!" Maggie jumped to her feet and lost herself in his laughing blue eyes. Regardless of what others would think, Maggie threw her arms around Garrett's neck.

Garrett exchanged a smile over Maggie's back with Jason. Both men silently acknowledged the transfer of Maggie's care from Jason to Garrett.

Garrett held Maggie tightly and could hardly contain his happiness. His Maggie loved him.

Maggie pulled herself away, becoming aware for the first time of the man standing behind Garrett. She lowered her eyes and blushed at the thought of this man overhearing her words of endearment.

Garrett's soft chuckle told Maggie he understood her sudden silence. "This is David Monroe, our local preacher."

Maggie raised her eyes and took the hand David offered her.

"I'm pleased to meet you, Miss Intissar."

"Please call me Maggie. I'm pleased to meet you too. My father has nothing but the highest praise for you," Maggie said and turned to her father. "Look who's here, Father. It's Garrett and Pastor Monroe."

Jason nodded ever so slightly.

"I'll agree to call you Maggie, but you must drop the formalities and call me David," the blond man said, smiling broadly at her. Maggie liked him immediately and soon forgot her discomfort.

"Agreed," she declared.

"Maggie, I'd like to speak to you," Garrett said, taking her arm. "In private." Maggie looked first to David, then to her father.

"Father, I need to speak with Garrett. Will you be alright?" she questioned, fearing if she left him for even a moment, something might go wrong.

"I'll be fine. I want to talk to David anyway," Jason assured her. Maggie nodded, wondering if David would offer her father comforting images of eternity in heaven. As she walked into the hallway with Garrett, she strained to hear their words.

"Did you hear me, Maggie?" Garrett questioned in a whispered hush.

"What?" Maggie asked, turning to see a concerned Garrett.

"There's no easy way to tell you this, but Miguel is dead."

CHAPTER 18

"How? Where?" Maggie asked, her mind flooding with questions.

"Banditos," Garrett replied. Maggie shivered uncontrollably. She felt cold and dizzy. Concerned, Garrett put an arm gently around her and said, "Come with me to the library and we'll talk."

Maggie tried to make her feet work, but her brain refused to function. She sat where Garrett directed her to sit, not knowing what to say.

Garrett sat across from Maggie and told the story. "Miguel never made it to the mission. When Mack showed up and told me about the butchered steers, I figured there wouldn't be good news about Miguel. We looked for signs of him on the trail, but there was nothing. Then we decided to take a look at the water hole where you found the carcasses. We found Miguel at the bottom of the pond."

"Dear Lord." Maggie breathed the words, and Garrett knew they were a prayer all their own.

"We buried him. We couldn't bring him back here in the shape he was in."

Maggie nodded dumbly. She suddenly realized she had been at the site of Miguel's murder. While she had sat on Thunder, Miguel had lain dead at the bottom of the water hole. The room began to spin.

"I'm so sorry, Maggie," Garrett offered softly. "I know this is difficult. There was no easy way to tell you." Again Maggie nodded and said nothing. Garrett continued talking, but Maggie's mind went to Carmalita.

"Oh, Garrett," she interrupted. "What about Carmalita? Does she know?"

"I told Maria. She said she'd break the news to her," Garrett replied, rubbing the back of his neck.

Garrett was dusty and sweat soaked, but Maggie had never known a more welcome sight. God had sent him back safely to her. She offered a silent prayer of thanksgiving for Garrett's safety, but she couldn't forget Carmalita's sorrow.

Slowly she got to her feet. "I'll have Maria prepare you a bath. I must go to Carmalita." With that Maggie turned and went in search of the two women.

Garrett stared after Maggie for several minutes. He was amazed at the change in her. Where once had been a childish young girl, now stood a woman. A woman who compassionately put her pain aside to tend to the hurts of others. Garrett smiled. His Maggie had grown up.

Maria went to draw a bath for Garrett, but she could offer Maggie little help in locating Carmalita. Maggie looked throughout the ranch house but found no sign of the missing girl. She searched the quiet courtyard without success.

Maggie finally made her way to Carmalita's room. When there was no response to her knock, she quietly opened the bedroom door. A single lantern burned on the night stand, but Carmalita was gone.

Maggie returned to her father's room and found him listening to David Monroe read from the Psalms. Knowing what comfort her father found from the Bible, she decided against disturbing them and went to seek out Garrett.

Garrett sat refreshed behind Jason's large walnut desk. He was dividing his attention between a cup of black coffee and a ledger book when Maggie arrived.

"I can't find Carmalita!" Maggie's voice betrayed the worry she felt. Garrett looked up from the papers.

"Have you looked everywhere?"

Maggie nodded. "I checked the entire house. Oh, Garrett. I'm worried. Miguel was everything to Carmalita. Where could she be?"

Garrett pushed the papers aside and grabbed his coat. "I'll check the barn and the corrals. You stay put. I'll be back shortly."

Maggie paced the room until she was certain she'd worn a hole in the heavy Indian rug. She tried to sit, but her mind was consumed with worry and grief. Just then, Garrett came rushing into the room.

"She took a horse. I've a feeling she's gone to find where we buried Miguel," Garrett announced.

Maggie rushed to where Garrett stood. "But it's dark and growing colder by the minute."

"I've sent a couple hands after her. I felt it was important for me to stay. I hope that's okay with you."

"Oh yes, Garrett. Please don't leave me again." For once, Maggie didn't try to hide her tears. Garrett took her into his strong arms.

"Hush, now. I'm here and I'm not going anywhere — at least not without you," he added softly.

"Señor, Señorita." Maria burst into the room, panting from her hard running.

"What is it, Maria? Have you found Carmalita?" Maggie asked as she rushed to Maria's side.

"I found this," Maria said, holding up a piece of paper.

Garrett took the note from Maria. His eyes narrowed slightly as he read it.

"What is it, Garrett?" Maggie questioned anxiously.

"It says Carmalita knows who killed Miguel. She's gone to avenge Miguel's death," Garrett spoke gravely. "I'll have to go, Maggie. Maria, go find Bill for me, and hurry."

"Sí." Maria was still breathless, but she sped from the room.

"Garrett, you can't go! What if it's a plot? What if they want to kill you?" Maggie cried.

Garrett unlocked the gun cabinet. "I can't expect Carmalita to face banditos on her own. She's probably unarmed, and a lone woman approaching a rowdy bunch like that? Well, I'd rather not say what I'm thinking."

Garrett opened the cabinet and took out a rifle and some cartridges. Maggie crossed the room to his side.

"Please don't go. Send someone else." She was crying. Garrett placed the rifle and cartridges on the table and took Maggie in his arms.

"Shh, don't cry. It's going to be alright. We might even catch up to her before she gets very far." Garrett stroked Maggie's damp cheek, knowing the tears she cried were from love for him.

Maggie lifted her face to Garrett's and looked deep into his eyes. She saw his resolve. "I love you, Garrett," she whispered.

"Maggie, you can't know how I've dreamed of hearing you say that. I've waited a lifetime for you. I love you, and I'm not going to do anything foolish to risk the happiness I know we'll share." With those words, Garrett leaned down and kissed her. It was a long and loving kiss. A kiss that left Maggie flushed and breathless.

"Garrett," Maggie's voice still held the urgency she felt. "Let's pray together before you go."

Garrett smiled. "I can't think of anything more necessary," he answered. Taking down a well-worn Bible from the fireplace mantel, Garrett turned to Psalm 91. " 'He that dwelleth in the secret place of the most High,' " Garrett read, " 'shall abide under the shadow of the Almighty. I will say of the

Lord, He is my refuge and my fortress: my God; in Him will I trust. Surely He shall deliver thee from the snare of the fowler, and from the noisome pestilence. He shall cover thee with His feathers, and under His wings shalt though trust: His truth shall be thy shield and buckler.' "

Garrett replaced the Bible and knelt with Maggie. "Father, we seek Your guidance. You know the situation and our need better than we do. We ask that You cover us in Your protection. Protect Carmalita too, Father. She's out there somewhere. We don't know where — but You do. Place a shield of protection around her. In Jesus' name —"

"Wait," Maggie interrupted. "Father, please watch over Garrett. I know I've been a stubborn child in the past, but Garrett has sought Your will for a long, long time. I know he places his trust in You. Sometimes it's hard for me to trust, but I know You love him even more than I do. Please bring him safely back to me. In Jesus' name. Amen."

"Amen," Garrett added and squeezed Maggie's hand. "And to think," he smiled. "I get to share this with you for a lifetime."

Maggie smiled too. "I feel better. Now I can let you go without fearing the worst."

Getting to her feet with Garrett's help, Maggie laughed nervously.

"What?" Garrett asked.

"I wish I had a piano."

"A piano?" Garrett responded. "What does that have to do with anything?"

"Back in Topeka, whenever things got bad or I felt lonely, I would pound out my frustrations on the piano. It helped to pass the time, and it soothed my nerves." Maggie smiled and looked around the room. "Father bought me a wardrobe full of clothes, but there isn't a single piano on the ranch." She feigned utter misery.

Garrett laughed and whirled Maggie in a circle. "You shall have the best and finest piano money can buy for a wedding gift from me," he said as he finally let Maggie's feet touch the ground. "Though I haven't the slightest idea how we'll get it here." At this they both laughed.

Bill came rushing into the room, knowing the gravity of the situation from Maria's brief explanation. He was somewhat confused to find Garrett and Maggie laughing. He cleared his throat to gain their attention.

Garrett was the first to sober. "Bill, we've got to go after Carmalita." Maggie grew solemn.

Bill nodded his head. "Maria told me. I've got ten men who'll ride with us."

"Good. Then let's be at it," Garrett replied.

"There's somethin' else you ought to know, Boss."

"What?" Garrett questioned.

"The boys finished a head count on the stock. We're short nearly a hundred steers."

"A hundred? Are you sure?"

Maggie didn't like the tone of Garrett's voice. Something in Bill's statement had signaled more danger, of this she was certain.

"They're sure alright. Herd's been down from the hills for over a week. Them that we didn't sell, we turned loose on the ridge. Since I saw signs of snow, I had the boys bring 'em on down. After we got 'em all corralled, we counted about ninety-eight missing."

"What does this mean, Garrett?" Maggie asked.

"Most likely rustlers," he replied and went to the desk to retrieve the rifle and ammunition.

"Rustlers and banditos? And poor Carmalita out there? Please be careful, Garrett." Maggie's voice quivered as she placed her hand on his arm.

"I will. Keep praying." Then he kissed her and was gone.

CHAPTER 19

Maggie went silently to her father's room. David was reading the Bible in a gentle, even tone. Silently, Maggie took up her knitting and sat in a chair across the room. The words David recited offered her comfort as no others could.

David sensed something was wrong, but he knew better than to disturb Jason's rest by asking questions.

After an hour, Maggie could no longer sit still. "Excuse me, David. I think we should let Father sleep now." David nodded, sensing the urgency in Maggie's voice.

"Jason," David said. "I'll be in the kitchen trying to talk Maria out of her spectacular custard. If you need me, just give a holler."

"Thank you, David. You've been a comfort, but Maggie's right. Sleep will do me good." Jason's words were hoarse whispers.

"Father, do you need more medication?" Maggie knew it had been several hours since his last dose of morphine.

"No, no. I feel surprisingly better. You run along and fix David up with something to eat. I'm fine, child. Really." Jason raised his hand weakly to flag them on their way. Maggie took hold of it.

"I love you, Father. I'll be close by. You just rest."

Maggie led David to the kitchen, but Maria sent them off to the dining room, promising to serve them her best custard.

"Things aren't as they should be," Maggie began as David helped her with her chair.

"I thought as much, but I didn't want to worry your father. He's perceptive for a sick man."

"A dying man," Maggie murmured.

"Yes, that's true. Hard to believe though," David declared. "I've never met a man who lived life to the degree your father has." David paused as he studied Maggie. It was easy to see why Garrett was drawn to her. "Has your father told you about the mission?"

"A bit here and there. Until a short time ago, we weren't on speaking terms. And I wasn't on listening terms, either. I missed a great deal of time with him because of my stubbornness."

"You can't live your life under a rock of

regrets. We all have things we wished we'd done differently. Some things we wish we hadn't done at all, but what's done is done. We seek God's forgiveness, change our ways, and make amends. You're doing a fine job, Maggie. It's clear you've brought him happiness."

Maria entered the room and placed two warm bowls of custard on the table. Moments later, she returned with David's favorite caramel sauce.

"You spoil me, Maria. But I love it." David laughed and ran a hand through his straight blond hair.

"Thank you, Maria. It looks wonderful," Maggie added.

"Don't tell me you've never had Maria's caramel custard?" David asked, a look of disbelief on his face.

"I might have and not remembered. Not much of the past few months registered. I was so angry. I could have eaten about anything and never known."

"Mostly, Señorita didn't eat at all," Maria stated matter-of-factly.

"That's true," Maggie laughed. "Twice, Carmalita had to alter my clothes. Poor Carmalita," Maggie's voice sobered.

"What is it?" David questioned.

"Carmalita took off after the people who

killed Miguel. She left a note saying she knew who was responsible. Garrett rounded up some men and took off after her."

"It's awfully cold and dark out there," David began. "But Garrett knows every inch of this land. If anyone can find her, he can. But I'm sure glad I didn't ask about this while we were with your father."

"Yes," Maggie said, tasting the custard. "Maria, this is wonderful!"

"Gracias, I'm glad you like it. I'll be in the kitchen if you need me."

Maggie nodded and continued explaining to David. "On top of everything else, some cattle are missing. It seems the rustlers and banditos are plotting to destroy us."

Just then, Maria came rushing into the room. "Señorita, Señorita! You must come quickly."

"What is it, Maria?" Maggie said as she followed Maria to the kitchen door. David was close behind the women.

Maria opened the door to admit a young Mexican boy. He looked twelve or thirteen, and Maria introduced him as her grandson. "He lives in the mountains," Maria added, admitting to his life with the banditos.

Maggie looked back and forth from Maria to the young boy. "Well? What is it?" Maggie asked, no longer able to contain her concern.

The boy rattled off in Spanish, and while David nodded his understanding, Maggie didn't know what was being said. When the boy finished delivering his message, David interpreted it for Maggie.

"He says his people didn't butcher your cattle. He's been sent here by his parents because they knew his grandmother would protect him," David explained. Then he turned and questioned the boy.

The boy answered hesitantly, but his response satisfied David. "He says the banditos would never harm Señor Jason's hacienda. He's been very good to them, and that is why they've sent word to you. They don't want to be blamed for this."

"How did they find out about it?" Maggie questioned.

"They found the mess at the water hole. They knew someone had made it look like banditos were to blame." David answered. "They wanted to vindicate themselves."

Suddenly, Maggie grew cold. If Carmalita knew the person who had killed Miguel and it wasn't done by banditos, then the murderer had to be someone on the ranch. As if reading Maggie's mind, David instructed Maria to have her grandson stay the night and to lock all the doors and windows.

"David, the killer could be riding with Garrett right now," Maggie sobbed. "I can't lose him." She started for the door, but David held her fast.

"I can't let you go, Maggie. You know that, and you know why. Now come with me, and we'll sit with your father," David said firmly.

"But what of your wife?" Maggie asked. "Will she be safe at the mission?"

David's jaw tightened. "Let's go sit with Jason."

The hours passed, and Maggie struggled to appear at ease in front of her father. David had started reading the Bible once more, and Maggie wondered if he were doing so in part to answer his fear for Jenny.

Jason had fallen into a deep sleep, so David put aside the Bible and stretched his long legs by walking to the bedroom window.

"If you like, I could show you to the guest room," Maggie offered. Her own body was suffering from the tension. She had considered retiring to her room, but she hated to leave David alone.

"No. I think we should stay together," David said, turning to meet Maggie's worried expression.

"Don't worry, Maggie. I've always been

overly cautious. It's one of my faults."

Maggie smiled. She knew David was trying to put her at ease. The wind picked up, and a light mist started to fall. Maggie listened to the rain grow heavy, then lighten again. She remembered times in Topeka when she'd sat in her room listening to the rain. She'd loved to snuggle down under the covers of her bed as the rain beat against the window panes. It had always made her feel safe. What she wouldn't give to feel safe now!

Uneasy, Maggie joined the others in fitful sleep. As the first light of dawn crept over the eastern mountains, Maggie and David were jerked awake by thundering horse hooves. Maggie glanced at her father, but he still slept soundly.

David went first to the window, then to the bedroom door. "Stay here," he ordered, and Maggie nodded. For once, she had no thought of disobeying orders.

She went to the window, anxious to see if she could catch sight of the riders. The scene revealed nothing. Maggie twisted her hands together. She paced back and forth at the end of her father's bed.

"Dear God, Garrett has to be alright. You have to keep him safe for me." Suddenly, her prayers sounded selfish. Maggie reconsidered her words. "Father, I know You have a plan for each of us. I can't imagine a plan for me without Garrett by my side, but I trust You. I believe You'll care for Garrett and for me in the best way. I give it over to Your will, Lord." Before Maggie could finish her prayer, voices in the hallway interrupted.

Maggie rushed to the door just as it opened. Garrett stood before her. Seeing that Jason was asleep, Garrett pulled Maggie into the hall and closed the door.

Maggie sobbed as she fell against Garrett's chest. "You're alright!" she whispered between her tears.

"Come with me, Maggie," Garrett said, refusing to let her go. They joined David in the living room. Garrett led Maggie to the high-backed sofa and had her sit beside him.

"Is it — did they?" Maggie couldn't bring herself to ask the questions on her mind. She was shaking from head to toe.

"It's over. At least for now," Garrett said softly, putting his arm around her in support.

"Carmalita?" Maggie dared to ask.

"She'll be staying at the mission while she recovers from all this," Garrett said. Noticing David's anxious expression, he added,

"Everything is fine there." David sighed in relief.

"We can talk about this later if you like," Garrett offered.

Maggie nodded, relieved that she wouldn't have to hear the details of what had taken place.

"I think I'll bid Jason good-bye and go home," David announced. "Jenny's bound to be beside herself."

Garrett nodded and added, "I had a couple men stay on until you get there."

A relieved look passed over David's face. "Thanks, Friend."

"I think I owe you thanks as well," Garrett replied. They shared a nod, each acknowledging the other's actions.

For a long time after David had left the living room, Maggie did nothing but allow Garrett to hold her. Silently, she thanked God over and over for bringing Garrett home safely. She praised Him for keeping Jenny and Carmalita safe too.

Just then, David returned. "Maggie," he said. "Your father is asking for you." Maggie dried her tears with her apron and followed David to her father's room.

"I'm here, Father. What can I do for you?" Maggie tried to smile as she knelt beside her father's bed.

Jason Intissar turned his weary blue eyes to the daughter he'd spent a lifetime loving. Behind her stood Garrett, arms folded across his chest, feet planted slightly apart.

"Father?" Maggie's small voice drew Jason's attention. "Is everything alright? Are you in pain?"

"No, Child. I called you here for something else." Jason paused to take a deep breath. "Maggie, I know I'm not going to live much longer. I thank God for these few moments with you, but I'm not a selfish man in respect to life. I've had a good one, and I'm ready to meet my God and your ma."

Jason stopped to draw another ragged breath. His body was seized by a fit of coughing, but to Maggie's surprise the spell lasted only a few moments.

"Father, you need to rest. We can come back later," Maggie said, getting to her feet.

Jason held out his thin hand. "Please wait."

"What is it, Father?"

"I have only one request, Maggie. Just one thing before I die," Jason said in uneven words. "I've already told David about it."

Maggie turned to meet David Monroe's tender eyes. She turned back to her father.

"I know a girl wants things a certain way

on her wedding day and you're deserving of that, but I want to see you married, Maggie. I don't have the time for a fancy wedding, and I'm asking a favor of you." Jason's words died off into a barely audible whisper. "I want you to marry Garrett here, today."

Maggie's heart lurched. She worried about hurting Carmalita by marrying so soon after Miguel's death. She also had no idea what Garrett had just been through. Perhaps he wouldn't want to get married right away. But her father's request was appropriate, and Maggie knew he didn't have much time.

Almost fearing the intensity of Garrett's eyes, Maggie turned to find him smiling. She blushed and lowered her eyes. Marriage to Garrett was what she'd dreamed of. It was hard to imagine in a few moments that dream would become reality.

Maggie turned back to her father. "I'd be happy to marry Garrett, right this minute, Father. Dresses, parties, and rooms full of people aren't as important as sharing this moment with you. If it meets with Garrett's approval, David can marry us this very minute."

Jason's face lit up with a huge smile.

"Well, what do you say, Mr. Lucas?" Maggie turned boldly toward Garrett. "Will you marry me?"

Forgetting the terror of the night and his deep concern for Maggie's safety, Garrett relaxed and even managed to laugh. "Are you proposing, Miss Intissar?"

Maggie joined his laughter. "Yes, I believe I am."

"In that case, I accept. But don't go getting any ideas about bossing me around in the future. This here is just a favor to Jason," he drawled, and everyone broke into laughter.

CHAPTER 20

While Maria was summoned to get Bill and Mack and anyone else who wanted to witness the event, David prepared for the wedding service. Garrett conferred with Jason in hushed whispers, and Maggie was suddenly alone.

She stood at the window, watching the rain. Rain was a bad omen on a wedding day. Maggie tried to remember the old saying. Something about the number of raindrops that fell would be the number of tears the bride would cry.

But, Maggie reminded herself, she didn't believe in bad luck. She believed in God's guidance. The rain was just rain.

"Scared?" Garrett's question was barely audible as he came up behind Maggie.

"A little — I guess," Maggie said. She looked up, slowly meeting Garrett's eyes — eyes so blue and powerful she felt herself grow weak.

"You haven't changed your mind, have you?" Garrett asked seriously.

Maggie's face shot up and her eyes flashed. "Never!"

"Then there's nothing to fear. We look to God for our future. I love you, Magdelena Intissar. I love you with all that I am." A tear slid down Maggie's cheek.

"I love you, Garrett Lucas. I can only pray I will be the wife you need," Maggie murmured. Garrett took her in his arms and held her tightly.

"Whoa, now. We haven't gotten to that part yet," David Monroe called from beside the fireplace. Everyone laughed and the tension broke.

Maggie joined hands with Garrett and stood at the foot of her father's bed. She glanced around the room at the ranch workers who'd become her friends. She only wished her mother and grandmother could have lived to see her wedding.

Maggie looked down at her attire and smiled, thinking how appalled her friend Lillie would have been at the blue calico dress. But Maggie knew Lillie would have liked Garrett.

Once or twice, Maggie gazed over her shoulder to find her father looking on, contentment beaming from his face. This moment was for him.

A few minutes later, David told Garrett he could kiss his bride. Garrett pulled Maggie close. His arms wrapped around her like a warm blanket. Their eyes met, and the promise of new life flashed before them. Then Garrett kissed Maggie deeply while the wedding guests cheered.

Jason held his hands up to Maggie and Garrett. "I've waited a long time for this day. I'm proud to call you son," Jason said, his eyes planted firmly on Garrett. "I'm trusting you to care for my daughter and to keep your family in line with the plans the good Lord has for you. This ranch and all I have is yours. Yours to share with Maggie." Garrett nodded and squeezed his father-in-law's hand.

"And my Maggie," Jason sighed. "How beautiful you are today. I want you to be happy. I want you to enjoy what I've made here, but most of all I want you to keep your heart close to God. I'm so glad I was here when you accepted Jesus as your Savior. I can go on now — knowing you're in God's care and Garrett's."

"Surprise!" Maria exclaimed as she re-entered the room. Maggie turned to see that Maria had brought refreshments.

"How wonderful!" Maggie cried, rushing

to Maria. "Our own reception."

Garrett joined his wife with a smile. "She's more interested in food than her new husband." Maggie blushed, suddenly aware she'd rushed from Garrett and her father to a tray of pastries.

Garrett laughed all the more at the sight of Maggie's embarrassment. "Well, I just thought it was kind of Maria," Maggie added, giving up at the roar of laughter from everyone.

The ranch hands didn't need second invitations to enjoy the treats. Maria poured steaming cups of Mexican coffee while the hands helped themselves to the tray of goodies.

David joined in the revelry. He had downed his third pastry by the time Maria offered him a cup of coffee. "These are some good eats, Maria. I wish Jenny had the recipe."

"I could write it down for her," Maria offered.

David nodded in appreciation. "You do that, Maria. I'd be much obliged."

Maggie had glanced over at her father once or twice. He was beaming. She was about to ask him if he wanted something to eat when Garrett asked her something.

"I'm sorry. I wasn't listening," Maggie

said apologetically.

"I was wondering if you thought this might be too much for your father. Maybe we should herd everybody out of here," Garrett whispered.

Maggie glanced around Garrett to where her father rested. Suddenly, her heart stopped. Color drained from her face, and she pushed past Garrett and ran to her father's bedside.

Jason still bore the smile Maggie had seen earlier, but his lifeless eyes betrayed the secret that he'd passed from one world to the next. Maggie placed his hand against her cheek, patting it gently.

"Father? Father, wake up," she cried, but in her heart she knew her father was dead.

Garrett and David were the only ones who noticed what was taking place. Garrett stood behind Maggie. He gently placed his hands on her shoulders. David moved to the opposite side of the bed and felt for a pulse. There was none.

"He's gone," David murmured softly.

It was only when David closed Jason's eyes that Maggie felt the impact of his words. Maria noticed what David was doing and quickly crossed herself and whispered a prayer. This caught the attention of the three ranch hands.

"He's past the pain now," Bill offered softly. "Mighty sorry to lose him, though. Mighty sorry." Maggie saw tears in Bill's eyes and heard his voice quiver. Bill had cared deeply for her father. Mack and Rob were silent, though Maggie noticed Mack turn to wipe his eyes with his sleeve.

Maggie moved away from Garrett and the bed, watching David tend to her father's body. Everything was moving in slow motion. Bill said something to Garrett, but Maggie couldn't make out the words. She couldn't hear anything over the pounding of her heart. The room began to swim, and desperately, Maggie reached out to steady herself. She saw Garrett look at her, then she collapsed at the foot of her father's bed.

Garrett rushed to lift Maggie in his arms. "Maria, get me a cold cloth."

"Sí, Señor," Maria said as she hastened from the bedroom.

"David, I've got to get her out of here," Garrett called over his shoulder.

"Don't worry about it. Take care of your wife," David answered. *My wife,* Garrett thought. After months of separation, they were finally married.

Garrett was moving toward the west wing of the house when he came across Maria.

"Come with me, Maria. We'll put her in my room."

Maria nodded and brought the basin of water and washcloth she'd gone for. She managed to balance the basin while opening the door for Garrett. He moved across the study that adjoined his bedroom, grateful that he'd left the bedroom door open. Maria followed, watching the tender way Garrett placed Maggie on the bed.

"Give me the cloth," Garrett requested. He placed the cloth across Maggie's forehead and began to pat her hand.

"Maggie, *mi querida,* wake up."

Maria moved forward to loosen the buttons at the neck of Maggie's gown. Maggie stirred slightly, and Garrett gently wiped her face with the damp cloth, hoping the coolness would bring her back to consciousness.

"Father," Maggie moaned softly. With a jerk, her eyes flew open. "No-o-o!" she cried. She struggled to sit up, but Garrett's firm hands held her back.

"Just rest a minute," insisted Garrett.

"Oh, Garrett," Maggie sobbed into her hands. Her body shook uncontrollably, and Garrett held her long after her tears had soaked the front of his shirt. "He can't be dead, Garrett! He can't be."

Maggie pulled back and turned her red, swollen eyes toward Maria. "Maria, please tell me he isn't dead."

But Maria found it hard to speak. She lowered her eyes, her own tears falling freely, and quickly left the room.

Maggie looked back to Garrett whose eyes were also wet with tears. "We'll all miss him," Garrett whispered.

It was then Maggie became aware of Garrett's pain. She steadied herself, studying the weary face of the man who was now her husband. The strain was as great on him as it was on her.

"Oh, Garrett, I'm so sorry. I know how you loved him," Maggie said, her heart filled with aching for the sadness she saw in Garrett's eyes. When tears began to roll down Garrett's cheeks, Maggie held him tightly. Together they shared their sorrow. It was not the wedding day either one would have planned, but their shared pain brought deeper intimacy to their marriage.

Two days later, Maggie joined Garrett beside the grave of her father. In torrential rain, Bill and Mack had taken turns digging the final resting place of their boss and friend. Maria had prepared Jason's body with David Monroe's help.

Garrett had finalized arrangements for the

last of the winter supplies to be brought in. He'd also handed the rustlers who had murdered Miguel over to the law.

Maggie had been horrified to learn that the rustlers' leader was Cactus Jack, her father's own ranch hand. Knowing her father was growing sicker and Garrett was nowhere around, Cactus Jack had figured they'd have a good chance of stealing lots of cattle.

The plan might have worked, but Carmalita had overheard pieces of a conversation between Cactus Jack and Miguel. Cactus Jack had wanted Miguel to join his operation, and when he'd refused, Cactus Jack had threatened his life.

With God's help, Garrett had been able to locate Carmalita before she'd found Cactus Jack and his men. Garrett had seen her safely to the mission and then turned his sights on collecting both his cattle and the rustlers responsible for their disappearance.

"It's time, Maggie," she heard Garrett saying. Maggie nodded somberly. She was grateful so many people were taking care of her. Everyone had pitched in. Maggie hadn't needed to lift a finger to help with the funeral or the ranch.

As she stood in the rain, watching little

rivers run down the side of the dirt mound that would soon cover her father's casket, Maggie shivered. Garrett quickly placed his coat around Maggie's shoulders. Maggie turned her eyes briefly to meet those of her husband.

Suddenly, she felt out of place. Garrett had his duties. Bill, Mack, and Maria all had their jobs. But Maggie's days of caring for her father were over, and she had nothing to do. Now that Carmalita was staying at the mission, Maggie didn't even have her to talk to.

Maggie glanced at the western ridge. She'd given up hope of Carmalita coming to the funeral. In this wet weather, the twelve mile ride to the ranch would be miserable for the heartiest ranch hand. Silently, Maggie chided herself for expecting Carmalita to put aside her grief over Miguel to attend the funeral.

Just as Maggie tried to concentrate on David's words, Carmalita came into view. Motionless, she looked down from the crest of a ridge, then nudged her horse to the valley and across to the ranch. She sat proudly, almost regally, in the saddle. David's words fell silent as all eyes turned to watch the stately procession. When Carmalita approached the graveside, Maggie left Garrett's side and went to her.

Pain and sorrow clouded Carmalita's face. "This," Carmalita said as she revealed a small pine wreath, "is for Señor."

Maggie reached up and took the gift. Dark green branches were intricately woven with red braided calico. Maggie appreciated the honor being paid to her father.

"Gracias, Carmalita," Maggie whispered, knowing further conversation would be meaningless. Maggie walked to the grave and lovingly placed the wreath upon her father's casket. Then she glanced back toward Carmalita. Carmalita nodded and started her horse back toward the mission.

"I'll miss her," Maggie whispered.

"We all will," Garrett said as he put his arm around his wife.

Maggie tried to focus on the words David had chosen to comfort those gathered for her father's funeral. " 'I am the resurrection, and the life: he that believeth in me, though he were dead, yet shall he live: And whosoever liveth and believeth in me shall never die,' " David quoted with love and assurance.

Maggie knew the words were true. Her father's death wasn't disturbing her as much as the feeling of being displaced. When David finished speaking, Maggie excused herself and moved to the house. Maria followed closely behind.

"Would you like some coffee or tea, Señora?" she asked in her thick accent.

"Thank you, Maria. I think I would like some coffee. I didn't sleep well last night," Maggie replied gratefully.

"Where will you take it?" questioned Maria as she shook the rain from her coat.

"Bring it to my room," Maggie began and then thought better of returning to her old bedroom. "No, please bring it to my father's room. I'd like some time alone." Maria nodded and left for the kitchen.

Maggie shook the rain from her coat and hung it to dry. She went to a small chest of drawers in the pantry and pulled out a fresh apron. During her father's illness, she had needed an apron's large, roomy pockets to carry a variety of things, but as Maggie tied the strings into a bow, she questioned her action.

I don't know why I'm putting on an apron, Maggie thought. *There's no one to nurse and nothing to do. I'm not needed.* Maggie walked to her father's room and sat in the rocking chair.

Maria had thoughtfully started a crackling fire that was warming the cool, damp air. Sitting opposite her portrait, Maggie studied the youthful image of herself. She remembered with sadness the hours she'd spent sitting for the portrait so her father would let her stay in Topeka.

Maria arrived with the coffee, but knowing Maggie wanted solitude, she did nothing more than pour a cup and leave.

Maggie sipped the dark liquid, enjoying the warmth that spread through her body. So many relationships had come to an end, but what of the gains? She had a new husband, but she wasn't sure what she was supposed to do with him.

Dear God, please help me to know my place and to find contentment in it. I feel so confused right now, Maggie prayed. *I want to belong, but with so many people I loved now gone, I don't know where to start. Please guide me, Lord. Teach me how to be a good wife.*

Garrett entered the room.

"Mind if I join you?" he drawled. Maggie could tell he was trying to be lighthearted.

"No, not really. At first I wanted to be alone, but not now," Maggie replied. Calm was beginning to spread through her soul, and Maggie knew her Heavenly Father was giving her peace.

"I'm glad," Garrett said, sounding old. "I need you." Maggie's eyes widened.

"You need me? Whatever for?" she questioned curiously.

"How can you ask?" Garrett inquired as he took a chair.

"Well, I have to confess I was feeling unnecessary. I don't know anything about the running of this ranch, and you have it all under control anyway. I'm not needed in the house — Maria manages nicely by herself. Winter is here, so there's little I can do outdoors. Even if I could go outside, what would I do?" Maggie asked.

She paused, studying the details of her father's now-familiar room. "When Father was alive, when he needed me to care for him, I knew I had a place to belong. I had a purpose."

"You think you have no purpose now?" Garrett questioned, contemplating Maggie's words.

"Yes," she admitted. "I suppose that sounds foolish, but there it is. I'm eighteen years old, and I feel so stupid. I don't know the first thing about being a rancher's wife. For that matter, I don't know much about anything."

"Come here, Maggie," Garrett ordered and motioned her with his finger. "Right now. Come here."

Maggie tilted her head and studied her husband. Setting her coffee aside, she walked slowly to where Garrett sat. When she stood beside him, Maggie could see tears in his eyes.

Garrett reached up and pulled Maggie to his lap. "I want you to listen, and listen good. Do you understand?" he questioned in a stern voice.

Maggie nodded. She could feel the warmth of his arms around her. It felt good to be held.

"A long time ago, I asked God to send me a wife. A helpmate, just like Eve was intended for Adam. I knew I wouldn't enjoy going through life without a companion. I never cared enough for my own company, I guess," he said with a little grin. Maggie smiled slightly.

"Fact is, I always saw myself with a woman by my side and children of my own. Family is mighty important to me, Maggie, especially because I lost mine at such an early age." Again Maggie nodded, but said nothing.

"God answered my prayer by sending you, and I praise Him daily for such a blessing. But I know nothing about being a husband except what the Bible tells me. By watching my own pa and yours, I saw what a father's heart was like. I learned to have the mind of a businessman and rancher. But I didn't learn anything about the heart of a husband. I'm starting from scratch, just like you."

Maggie's heart swelled at the deep love Garrett felt for her. She did belong. She belonged to God as His eternal child, and God had also blessed her with a husband — a husband who prayed for her. Maggie thanked God she belonged to Garrett.

"I understand," Maggie said with wonder. "It doesn't matter that I don't know the first thing about ranching or being a wife. What matters is I belong — we belong — to God and to each other."

Garrett held Maggie tightly and gazed steadily into her eyes. "That's all that matters, Maggie," he said with certainty.

"I love you, Garrett Lucas," Maggie whispered softly.

"And I love you, Maggie Lucas."

Outside, the rain poured harder than ever. Thunder echoed in the distance. But inside, two hearts had found shelter in the shadow of the Most High, a place to belong.

ABOUT THE AUTHOR

Tracie Peterson, best-selling author of over forty fiction titles and one nonfiction title, lives and works in Topeka, Kansas. As a Christian, wife, mother, and writer (in that order), Tracie finds her slate quite full.

First published as a columnist for the *Kansas Christian* newspaper, Tracie resigned that position to turn her attention to novels. After signing her first contract with Barbour Publishing in 1992, her first novel appeared in 1993 under the pen name of Janelle Jamison, and the rest is history. She has over twenty-three titles with Heartsong Presents book club and stories in six separate anthologies from Barbour, including the best-selling *Alaska.* From Bethany House Publishing, Tracie has several historical series, as well as a variety of women's fiction titles.

Voted favorite author for 1995, 1996, and 1997 by the Heartsong Presents readership, Tracie enjoys the pleasure of spinning stories for readers and thanks God for the imagination He's given. "I find myself blessed to be able to work at a job I love. I get to travel, study history, spin yarns, spend time with my family, and hopefully glorify God. I can't imagine a more perfect arrangement."

Tracie also does acquisitions work for Barbour Publishing and teaches workshops at a variety of conferences, giving workshops on inspirational romance, historical research, and anything else that offers assistance to fellow writers.

See Tracie on the Internet at http://members.aol.com/tjpbooks/

The employees of Thorndike Press hope you have enjoyed this Large Print book. All our Thorndike and Wheeler Large Print titles are designed for easy reading, and all our books are made to last. Other Thorndike Press Large Print books are available at your library, through selected bookstores, or directly from us.

For information about titles, please call:

(800) 223-1244

or visit our Web site at:

www.gale.com/thorndike

To share your comments, please write:

Publisher
Thorndike Press
295 Kennedy Memorial Drive
Waterville, ME 04901

R ¹ᴹ/₀₉   mc   R ¹/₀₇